OVERKILL

"Lacey Brighton went to the victim's house and viciously stabbed Celeste Shephard fourteen times." Walking close to Judge Campbell, her voice became hard. "Fourteen times. Three of the wounds were sufficient to end Ms Shephard's life, but the stabbing went on and on and on. Your Honor, this was more than murder. It was overkill."

POINT CRIME

OVERKILL

Alane Ferguson

■SCHOLASTIC

Scholastic Children's Books,
Scholastic Publications Ltd,
7-9 Pratt Street, London NW1 0AE, UK

Scholastic Inc.,
555 Broadway, New York, NY10012-3999,
USA

Scholastic Canada Ltd,
123 Newkirk Road, Richmond Hill,
Ontario, Canada L4C 3G5

Ashton Scholastic Pty Ltd,
PO Box 579, Gosford, New South Wales,
Australia

Ashton Scholastic Ltd
Private Bag 94407, Greenmount, Auckland,
New Zealand

First published in the UK by Scholastic Publications Ltd,
by arrangement with Bradbury Press,
an affiliate of Macmillan Inc. USA, 1993

Copyright © Alane Ferguson, 1992

ISBN 0 590 55401 8

Typeset by Quadraset Ltd, Midsomer Norton, Avon
Printed by Cox & Wyman Ltd, Reading, Berks

To my father, Edward Joseph Skurzynski,
for his wisdom and love

1

The man tugged at his stocking mask and crouched lower in her closet. A piece of wire hung coiled in his hand; his breath came shallow, ragged.

Lace from a nightgown ruffled in a summer breeze, wrapping around the girl's legs as she danced to notes from a silver music box. Her hair was long and smooth, gilded by some distant light, and she twirled, spun, then floated until the music left and she heard the harsh breathing of the man. Puzzled, the girl watched the closet door open, so slowly. She tried to scream, tried to run, but stood frozen. The man snapped the wire taut; as he raised his hand to strike she saw the flash of an ax blade . . .

Lacey jerked awake. Moonlight illuminated her

room, bathing its edges in soft light and shadow. The doors of her closet were shut tight, like the lid of a box. Nothing was there. No one was there.

Another nightmare.

Trembling, she pulled a knot of covers under her chin. Her skin felt cold, clammy. Take a deep breath, she told herself, just like her therapist had instructed. Let it out slowly. Anxiety. That's what Mr Otkin said she had. Inhale, pause, exhale. Relax your hands; let the tension flow out of each fingertip; out of your feet, out of your calves and thighs.

Remember, dreams are the way your subconscious mind lets go of fear. Inhale, hold, now exhale as though you're blowing steam from a bowl of hot soup. Clear your thoughts. Don't think about the dance recital. Don't think about Celeste. Don't think about anything – just relax. As her heart began to slow, Lacey felt the coil of emotion gradually unwind. These dreams that haunted her night after night seemed so real, but she'd been told they were nothing more than poor test grades and family worries. With one more glance at her closet, she rolled onto her stomach, closed her eyes, and sighed deeply. Moments later, Lacey Brighton was asleep.

School began as usual. She was late.

"Where have you been?" Sean Nolan asked as

Lacey hurriedly pulled folders from her locker. "We were supposed to study before class, which is now going to start in . . ." He glanced at his watch. "Exactly five minutes."

"I'm sorry, okay? I overslept. Are you ready for the test? Never mind – what was I thinking!" She smacked her palm to her forehead. "Of course you are! Let me just grab my book . . ."

Placing his hands on her shoulders, Sean turned Lacey until she faced him squarely. His eyes, deep set and coffee brown, squinted slightly as he looked down on her five-foot-two-inch height. "Lacey, right now you've got a D in Social Science. A *D!* You have got to bring it up or . . ."

Jerking away, Lacey kicked her locker shut. "Knock it off, Sean."

"We're seniors, Lacey. Our grades count. You've *got* to quit screwing around!"

"Let me remind you that you're my *boyfriend*, not my warden and *not* my mother. Besides," she said, softening her tone when she saw his eyes flash, "I've been busy working on my dance performance, which is giving me nightmares. I've never had the lead before and – rats, there's the bell."

At the sound of the first bell, students scurried like roaches caught in sudden light. Sean stood, unmoving, his eyes locked on hers. Finally he said, "You can't talk your way out of a test, Lace.

That's all I'm saying. But you do whatever you want."

"I'll be fine. Really! Don't worry so much. Life's short."

She felt a pang of guilt as she hurried beside Sean down the hall. It was just like him to ride her about her grades. A straight-A student, Sean never could understand the way Lacey ran her life. In some strange way her life was like a gamble: gamble that there'd be no quiz that day, gamble that she'd find a last-minute parking spot, gamble she could pull it off.

Sometimes she'd win, sometimes she'd lose, but at least she didn't march in formation like the rest of them. Like Sean.

"Lacey Brighton, I'd like to see you today after class," Mrs Hernandez said, her voice crisp. She slipped a test, ink side down, onto Lacey's desk top. Pulling back a corner, Lacey sneaked a peek at last week's quiz. "D –" was scrawled across the top in angry red ink.

"What'd you get?" Sean asked in a loud whisper.

"A grade."

"Pretty bad, huh?"

"Yeah – happy?"

"No talking!" Mrs Hernandez warned. During the rest of class, while she racked her brain for answers on the test she hadn't studied for, Lacey formed the excuses she'd give Mrs Hernandez. Her teacher would have to understand the dance rehearsals Lacey was involved in, which of course took extra time and concentration. It was perfectly natural that some of her study time would slip. She could always throw in the fact that her mother was going away on yet another business trip; the emotional strain of being left alone took its toll. She'd stress the personal problems, she decided. Go for the sympathy.

But one look at Mrs Hernandez's face told her that excuses would get her nowhere. Shuffling through a stack of papers, Mrs Hernandez gave them a nasty snap and then began to speak before Lacey could say a word.

"Lacey, perhaps you aren't aware of this, but I taught your sister, Sara, in this very classroom eight years ago. You Brighton girls are smart, but for a reason I can't fathom, you, Lacey, think you can bull your way through my class."

Cheeks flaming with humiliation, Lacey looked at the ground. Dirt from one of Mrs Hernandez's plants had spilled from her desk top to the floor, and it made an interesting pattern against the beige tile.

"I'm aware you have only a short time between classes, so I'll make this brief. As of right now you're within a hair's breadth of flunking Social Science. I like you, Lacey. I really do. You're bubbly, you're fun. You're a very nice person. For that reason and because I admire your sister so much, I'd like to give you a chance to improve your grade. As you know we're about to tackle a unit on our American legal system, and since Sara is a lawyer, practicing right downtown . . ."

"No!" Lacey cried, her head shooting up. "We, Sara and I, don't get along much and . . ."

Folding her arms across her chest, Mrs Hernandez interrupted, "Whatever your problems, I hope for the sake of your grade that you'll be able to iron them out. It would be an enriching experience for our class, and I'm sure Sara would love helping you with a report. I could arrange for a pass so that you'd sit in on an actual trial." Her teacher's hair, dark and streaked with gray, hung over her shoulders. She flipped it onto her back and added, "Extra credit like this would increase your overall grade to at least a C, maybe even a B. Think about it, Lacey. Come in after school if you're interested. That's all."

"Are you going to eat that orange?" Tamera asked.

"Take it." Lacey tossed the orange into her friend's outstretched hands. "I shouldn't eat anything anyway 'cause I'm being measured for my costumes today."

"So? What you need is more, Lace, not less."

Lacey looked down at her chest. "Thank you. Thank you very much."

"Stop it! That's not what I meant!" Tamera flung a crumpled napkin in Lacey's direction. "You look great and you know it!"

"I've worn a training bra for so long, my chest should be able to do tricks."

"*Lacey!*" Even though Tamera tried to look horrified, laughter exploded from behind her hands. Lacey knew she had her. Tamera always cracked up at Lacey's jokes, which was why she was so much fun to have around. She was an easy mark.

"What's so funny?" Sean asked, dropping beside Lacey on the cafeteria bench. He pulled the flip top from his Coke. "What'd I miss?"

"Never mind, Sean," Tamera told him, "it's a girl joke. I swear I never know what will come out of her mouth."

Lacey shook an auburn curl off her face. Small and thin-boned, she had what Tamera called a "dancer's body," which Lacey translated to mean flat-chested. Her large eyes were more brown than hazel; her mouth was full-lipped and her smile off-center.

Sean, Tamera, and Lacey had been eating lunch at the same table since the school year started. That's really the way they'd hooked up, Lacey thought. True love had sprung from a mound of runny mashed potatoes. Sean had taken his lunch tray, slid it right next to hers and asked, "Is this spot taken?" in such a nice way that she'd scooted across the bench to make room. His smile had been wonderful – so deep that commas formed at the sides of his mouth, and he dressed in casual but expensive clothing, straight out of an L.L. Bean catalogue. He'd never been heart-thumping handsome, just nice-looking. Black hair, clipped neatly at the sides, curled like wire on the top of his head. His nose was a shade long; his ears cupped forward ever so slightly.

"Hey, Lace, what did Hernandez say to you after class?" Sean wanted to know.

"Oh, that," Lacey moaned, munching a fistful of chips in the hubbub of the cafeteria. "She wants me to do a report on my beloved sister, Sara, patron saint of legal sleaze. Yuck!"

"Remember, Sara is different than you are, not better," Tamera offered.

"You sound just like Mr Otkin. 'Do not compare yourself with your sister, Lacey. Take a deep breath, now exhale! Relax and think: You are your own person!' I bet Otkin never had an overachiever for a sibling. It sure ruins the familial curve."

"I think doing this report is a great idea," Sean broke in. "You can make up for a whole quarter with just one project."

"*Please* do not get on my case about this, Sean. I don't want to have to listen to a lecture from Sara, and I sure can't handle one from you." Sticking an elbow into Tamera's side, Lacey said, "Hey, I need to go to the girls' room. How about you?" and gave Tamera "the look."

"Oh, yeah, I need to go, too," Tamera agreed. "We'll be back in a minute, Sean."

As the door to the rest room swung shut, Lacey collapsed against the blue-and-white tile wall. "You know, Sean has got to be the oldest seventeen-year-old I've ever met." She dropped her voice low and mimicked, " 'Lace, doing that report is a great idea! Lace, you really need to study more. Lace, you've got to quit screwing around.' He knows how I feel about my sister, but he keeps right on pushing!"

Tamera walked to the mirror, then rifled in her purse until she found her lip gloss and liner. Very carefully she applied a thin, pink line to her upper lip. "I know what you want me to say, Lacey." She paused to outline the bottom of her mouth, then added, "But for once I'm going to tell you what I think. Sean's right. You're an idiot if you don't take advantage of Hernandez's offer." Squeezing a dab of pink gloss onto her finger, she ran it over her lips and smiled. "Hasn't it occurred to you that you'll get a pass out of school? Your sister is bound to help – she couldn't stand it if you did a half-assed job. I'll bet she'd even type the bloody thing. What a deal!"

"I know," Lacey added, thoughtful. "And for sure this project would get me mileage with my mom, but . . . I just don't know." Tossing back a mane of curls, she stared at Tamera and asked, "Do you really think it's a good idea?"

"Absolutely."

"Even though it's Sara?"

"Even though it's Sara."

"Okay," Lacey said, grabbing the gloss from Tamera's hand. "You're right. I'll do it!"

2

Lacey Brighton watched her sister stand and shuffle papers at the defense table. The courtroom was only half-filled, but Sara Brighton looked as intense as if she were about to argue a case before the Supreme Court. A fan spun aimlessly against the ceiling, moving overheated air onto the heads of restless spectators. Lacey shifted in her seat. The backs of her knees were sweating. Although it was February and freezing outside, the courtroom sweltered. Something had gone wrong with the heating system in the courthouse.

"Due to the hour, and to the temperature of the room, I feel we should call a recess," the judge announced. A black woman with severe features, Judge Wilson's appearance was at odds with her soft, slightly Southern voice. "Do you have any objection to that, Ms Brighton?"

"Yes, I do, Your Honor. I would like to cross-examine this witness on one point of her testimony. It will only take a moment, and I believe it is important to ask the question now."

Shaking her head, Judge Wilson answered, "As long as you get right to the point. The ladies and gentlemen of the jury deserve a lunch hour. You may proceed."

It was an interesting case, and in spite of herself Lacey felt drawn into it. Sara's client, a tough-looking young man named Earl Craw, was charged with holding up a convenience store. He was so thickly muscled that when he hunched forward, the seams of his brown polyester jacket strained visibly. On the stand, waiting patiently for Sara's cross-examination, sat a fifty-something woman named Mona Tilborn. She had just finished testifying that Craw was the man who had robbed her.

Against the east side of the room nine women and three men stared solemnly from a jury box. The women fanned themselves with wilted paper; the men, apparently preferring to sweat, wiped at their foreheads with the backs of their hands. The heating system was to be fixed by that afternoon, Judge Wilson promised. "Fat chance," Sara had mouthed to Lacey.

Dressed in a coal-black suit and pearls, Sara was the only person in the room who looked cool. Thick, red-blond hair brushed against the collar of her silk blouse; other than coral lipstick and a dusting of powder, she wore no makeup.

"Ms Brighton," the judge said, her voice now crisp, "I suggest you finish gathering those papers and get on with it."

"Yes, Your Honor."

Lacey cringed, but her sister seemed unperturbed. Spinning on the heel of her black leather pump, Sara walked confidently to the witness stand. Mona Tilborn flashed a nervous smile and pulled on the tips of her fingers.

"Mrs Tilborn? I'm Sara Brighton. I'll be asking you a few questions about what happened on the night of November twenty-second. You identified my client as the person who robbed you." Sara swept her arm toward Earl.

"Darn right."

"And you say you recognize him as the man who put a gun to your cheek?"

Mona nodded eagerly in reply. "Yeah, like I said before, that's him. He goes, 'Lady, don't give me no trouble or I'll blow your brains right out'a your head.' No way would I forget his face." Half-moon eyebrows, carefully painted in black, jumped up and down Mona's forehead as she talked.

Sara moved closer. "And you were standing behind the cash register when this happened, were you not?"

Again an eager nod. "I sure as hell was."

"Where you'd been standing the entire night. You never moved from behind that register, not even for one moment?"

It was then that Lacey saw it. Mona's eyes flicked, just for an instant. "I guess."

"You guess what?"

"I don't remember."

"Let me repeat the question. Did you ever move from your position behind the counter?"

"I might have moved, sometime."

"So there were periods during the evening of November twenty-second when you were not at the cash register. What exactly were you doing when you weren't at your post?"

"I might have been straightenin' the shelves."

Weaving her fingers and placing them under her chin, Sara narrowed her eyes. It was a move Lacey was familiar with. It meant her sister's guns were loaded, and the person in her sights was about to get shot.

"Straightening the shelves." Sara glanced toward the jury, then back to Mona. "Straightening the shelves. Were these 'shelves' by any chance in the back room?"

"Yeah. So?"

"And did those very same 'shelves' happen to contain a bottle of Puerto Rican rum, rum which you drank, not just on the night in question, but on every night?"

Now Mrs Tilborn looked confused. Her eyes began to dart from side to side. "What?"

"I think you heard the question. Why don't you quit stalling and answer?"

"Objection!" cried the prosecutor. A small, birdlike man, he jabbed his pen in Sara's direction, protesting, "Defense is badgering the witness."

"Your Honor," Sara broke in, "I have evidence that Mona Tilborn drank alcohol while on duty the night of November twenty-second, and did, in fact" – she paused for effect – "drink every night she was employed at the convenience store."

There was a small gasp from the crowd. What looked to be a row of Mona's friends rippled their heads together in frantic whispers.

"What – can she say that, Judge?" Mona demanded.

"I have the sworn statements of two eyewitnesses. I can call them to the stand right now . . ."

"Witnesses!" the prosecutor exploded. "I haven't been informed of any witnesses!"

Waving papers through the air like white flags, Sara walked in front of the jury, then handed them to Judge Wilson. "With the court's permission,

I submit that this evidence brings the identification of my client as the man who robbed Mona Tilborn into serious doubt."

"Quiet in the courtroom!" the judge bellowed.

Lacey felt the crowd hush and lean forward hungrily. This was just the kind of blood they had come to see. The kind of blood her sister could supply.

After glancing through the papers, Judge Wilson stated, "Objection overruled. Answer the question, Mrs Tilborn."

"I . . . sure I took a nip every once in a while, but that's got nothing to do with what I know. That man said he was gonna kill me . . ."

"Is this before or after you became drunk?"

"*Objection!*"

With a slight bow to the prosecutor, Sara said, "Never mind. I withdraw the question."

Judge Wilson banged her gavel and scowled so deeply, furrows formed between her eyes. "The court will take a one-hour recess, and counsel will refrain from any more theatrics. Mrs Tilborn, you're excused. That is all."

As Sara turned, Lacey saw a smile curl at the edge of her lips. Sara Brighton, lawyer triumphant.

"Lace, wait up! I thought we'd grab a bite to eat while you interview me. Is cafeteria food okay?"

"Fine."

"I saw you sitting there in the back row, and then you just disappeared. How's the therapy going? Are you still seeing Mr Otkin?"

"Yep."

"That's good. Hey, you look nice today. Except you're wearing a shade too much makeup. Redheads like us should wear brown mascara, not black."

"Speaking of the color black, have you quit smoking yet? I was picturing your lungs . . ."

"All right, forget it, I'll mind my own business." Sara laughed.

As they walked down the hallway, Lacey noticed how easy it was to tell the lawyers from the rest of the people. Overweight and rumpled men and women walked close to the walls, leaving the center of the hallway free; it somehow reminded Lacey of the way cars moved to the shoulder of the road when an ambulance screamed by.

At the row of elevators, Sara and Lacey stood among a sea of suits and expensive cologne. The elevator doors slid open; the society of lawyers stepped in. Pollini briefcases and Louis Vuitton purses bumped Lacey, until the knot of people thinned one by one. The ride down was utterly silent.

"You haven't said much about my performance," Sara mentioned when they finally got off on the bottom floor. The basement of the courthouse had been converted to a crowded, smoke-filled cafeteria. "I don't know why, but I had this crazy idea you might be impressed."

"You were great."

"But?"

"But . . ." Lacey didn't know if she should tell what was bothering her. After they settled in, she plucked at her napkin, then opened her spiral notebook to a fresh page. Rolling her pen between her fingers, she looked at Sara. "Okay, you were right about some things bothering me. What I want to know is, did Earl do it or not?"

Sara fumbled in her purse for a cigarette, lit it, then inhaled deeply.

"What do you think?"

"Me? I think Mrs Tilborn was telling the truth, but I'm not sure the jury will believe her. Not after what you said about her being a drunk."

Taking another drag, Sara blew the smoke through her nostrils. "Let's hope you're right."

"Then Earl Craw is innocent?"

Sara planted her hand on top of Lacey's paper, fanning her fingers across it like a spider's web. "What I tell you now can't be in your report. I'd like you to understand how the system works, so I'll give you an honest, off-the-record answer. As my sister." She looked at her pointedly, then asked, "Can I do that? Can I talk to you in confidence?"

Nodding, Lacey fought to control a swell of

anger. It always infuriated her when Sara said, "Can I do that?" as though Lacey were an infant.

"I know this will sound a bit strange to you, but . . ." Her voice dropped. "The fact is, Earl Craw robbed that store. He's as guilty as sin."

Lacey leaned forward until her elbows practically touched her sister's. In an exaggerated whisper, she asked, "Then why are you trying so hard to get him off?"

Cutting the air with her cigarette, Sara said, "Because that's the way it works. We have what's called an adversary system of justice. I fight like hell, the prosecutor fights like hell, and then the one who convinces the jury they're right wins. It's as simple as that."

"Where does justice fit in?" Lacey picked up her pen, drew the number one, and circled it.

"Justice?" Sara's laughter sounded harsh. "Not very well, I'm afraid. But before you start foaming at the mouth, you've got to remember we have the best system in the world—"

"If you're guilty."

"No, if you're the one accused of a crime." Sara crushed her cigarette in a dirty ashtray, then shrugged. "Look, Lacey, if the prosecutor loses in there, it's because he didn't do his job. It's his fault, not mine. You might think it's distasteful to bring up things like Mona Tilborn's drinking, but that could be the very tactic that wins the case. And winning," she said, stabbing her salad with her fork, "is the name of the game. Now, let's eat our lunch and move off this subject for a moment. Mom mentioned your grades have slipped. How far down are you?"

"I'm eating lunch with a lawyer. I don't know how much further down I could go."

"Don't start with the lawyer jokes, Lacey. I'm not in the mood."

"Hey, you're into animal rights. Did I tell you that scientists are no longer experimenting on rats in their laboratories? Instead of rats, they're using lawyers. There are three reasons for this change. One . . ." Lacey held up her index finger. "If you use a lawyer, there's no public outcry."

Sara rolled her eyes.

"Two, the researchers don't become attached."

"Oh, pleeze," Sara groaned.

"And three, there are more lawyers in this country than rats, anyway. Get it? I love it!"

"Very funny, Lacey, but, I'm not going to bite. The subject we were on was your schoolwork. You know I'm here for you. I'll help you anytime! Why won't you let me in on your life?"

Sara's voice faded in the background as Lacey carefully unwound the paper from her straw. It wasn't necessary to pay attention. The dialogue from this point on would be the same. "You're an underachiever, Lacey. You should try harder. How can you ever hope to reach your full potential when you don't study?" And of course, Lacey's favorite line, "This is life, sweetie. This is not a dress rehearsal." If it weren't for her failing grade, there would be no way on earth that Lacey would be here. The funny part was, Sara didn't have any idea how much Lacey despised her lectures. But that was just like her sister – barge ahead and assume that her words were pearls to be gathered up and cherished.

". . . do well *now*. This is not a dress rehearsal, you know. And quit chipping your nail polish off your fingers while I'm talking. It makes me think you're not listening."

"Huh? Oh, sorry. Listen, Sara, I know how busy you are. You have helped me out so much. The problem is, I'm really not sure how to put it all together. Rehearsals are a bear right now. You know how Celeste disappeared? Tamera had to step in and take over her part, and I've had to help her every single day."

"Have you heard anything at all from Celeste?"

"No." Lacey hoped the sound of her voice would make Sara drop the subject, but it didn't.

"You realize this fight you two are having is making it very awkward for Mom. She's got to work with Celeste's mother all the time, and . . ."

Lacey's mind wandered again as Sara took off on another soliloquy.

When Lacey thought about it now, it was hard to believe that she and Celeste had ever been close. Three weeks ago, their friendship had suddenly died.

They'd first met at the Wilford Club, a place where designer perfume mingled with sweat, and middle-aged skin looked as smooth as polished leather.

"Lace," her mother had said, "I want you to be especially nice to Mrs Shephard. She's got the kind of connections that can make or break my new business. And be a good friend to her daughter, Celeste. I hear she's absolutely beautiful, like a perfect little Barbie doll." Her mother had pulled out a lipstick case and checked her smile in its mirror. She'd rubbed a rose-colored smudge off her front tooth.

"Why do I have to come along?" Lacey had wailed. "I hate business. I hate tennis."

"You're here because Elaine Shephard asked you to be here and landing Ms Shephard as a partner will keep a roof over our heads. Your father hasn't sent us any money. Keeping his bleached bimbo happy seems to have drained his bank account."

Lacey had cringed. Her mother never used to talk that way. The divorce had changed her, had sharpened her into someone Lacey hardly recognized. Gone was the slightly rumpled mother who would safety pin a hem and apply mascara in the car. The woman who occupied her mother's body ran six miles a day and pulled her face up tightly between her palms when she thought no one was looking. Graying hair had been reborn as ebony.

"Why do I have to be friends with the daughter? I don't even know her."

"Because this is business," her mother had snapped as she pulled open a heavy brass door which bore THE WILFORD CLUB in Old English scroll. "Besides, now that I'm supporting this family, we don't have friends – we have prospective clients." She'd reached over and tucked Lacey's T-shirt into her shorts. Her face had softened as she'd added, "Sweetheart, I know this is difficult, but for my sake, for *our* sakes, would you *please* try to make this thing go?"

At that moment Elaine Shephard had swept into the foyer on a cloud of sophisticated confidence. Two steps behind came Celeste. Lacey had been struck by her large, indifferent eyes.

"And this must be Lacey," Mrs Shephard had cooed after she'd air-kissed Mrs Brighton's cheek. "You're adorable. I'm so pleased to meet you." Lacey's fingers had been gripped by Mrs Shephard's cool hand. "Why don't you two girls start up a game while your mother and I talk. Is that okay with you, Celeste?"

Celeste had nodded. Her blond hair had been smoothed into a ponytail, and her tennis whites dazzled.

They'd walked down the corridor in silence.

"Do you play?" Celeste had finally asked.

"What – tennis? No, not much. Do you?"

"Yes."

There was a pause. Celeste led the way to the indoor courts. She popped open a fresh can of tennis balls and handed one to Lacey.

"Look – Stacey—"

"Lacey!"

"Whatever – you might as well know what the deal is. My mother thinks I'm antisocial to my peers. You've heard of my father, Jerold Shephard?"

Lacey shook her head no.

"Oh. Well, my father is a United States diplomat, and because of his position I spend most of my time with adults. It goes with the job. The point is, I don't choose to hang around kids my age, and that's got my mother worried. That's why you're here – she hopes we'll become instant friends."

Celeste dropped her racket down her back, then made a violent swing over her head. Her serve looked deadly. "Actually, my shrink says I'm not antisocial, I just don't 'connect with young people.' " She'd paused, then looked directly at Lacey. "I despise being pushed into friendships, don't you?"

"Absolutely," Lacey'd agreed, "I know exactly

what you mean. After my dad left us for a younger woman, my mom started Kaleidoscope Jewels and sort of drafted me into the business. Now my job is to act *perky* and *fun* for clients." Just a heartbeat later, Lacey had added, "And their kids."

"Your father left your mother for a younger woman?"

Lacey nodded. "Umm-hmm. Well, actually Angie's more of a girl than a woman. My dad went really crazy when he hit forty – and off-the-wall weird when he hit forty-five. First he got a motorcycle and then he got a hair transplant. My mom didn't mind him getting all that young stuff, until he got Angie. That's where she drew the line."

Lacey made a slicing motion with her hand. Celeste laughed.

"Did your dad and Angie marry?"

"No. They just live together."

"Do you like her?"

Shrugging, Lacey answered, "She's not too bad. The worst part is the way she talks." Lacey altered her pitch so that it became high and breathy. "Oh, Lacey, your dad is so totally awesome – I mean, he's just so incredibly *super*!" She bounced the tennis ball and caught it with one hand. "Angie is about as bright as a small appliance bulb."

Celeste had laughed again. Lacey had felt a warm glow spread inside. She'd broken through to

Celeste without compromising herself. Her mother would be pleased.

". . . and Mom is trying so hard, and, Lacey . . . are you listening to me?"

Lacey pulled herself back from her reflections. She looked at Sara. "Mom and Mrs Shephard. I heard you. Anyway, could you help me with the typing and stuff on my report for Hernandez? I thought maybe I could leave my notes with you." She smiled. "I'll really understand if you're too busy, but I know if you help me it'll get done right."

Sara tapped an unlit cigarette. Lacey dropped her eyes as she waited for her sister to answer.

"You really are a piece of work, you know that?" Sara asked. "Here you sit, so appalled with the way I do things, but you're still willing to roll over if I do your report."

"I'll do somersaults and flips if you'll help me." She looked up and gave Sara her most charming smile.

Sara sighed. "You win. I want you to do well in school, so I'll help you. You're a master manipulator, Lace, but you make the arm-twisting relatively painless. Okay, I'll organize these notes for you, and we'll get together at my apartment when you're ready to do the rest."

"Thanks," Lacey said. She smiled inside. There were still some things she did better than Sara.

3

"I see myself as a nice person. I really do. I have lots of friends . . . but she just somehow . . ." Lacey stopped and chewed on the end of her finger. Finally, she blurted, "Sara really gets to me!"

"You're nibbling your cuticle," said Mr Otkin. A fortyish man of nondescript features, Glade Otkin was as comforting to Lacey as a lullaby. Thinning, sand-colored hair had been painstakingly combed over a bald spot, and his ample middle seemed even softer under beige angora.

"You must try to break the old stress patterns," he told her gently. "Let me close these shades, and we'll begin." With a flick of his wrist, the shades snapped shut. "Breathe through your nose, that's it, a-a-and relax."

Once dimmed, the colors of the office faded into hues of honey and toast. A few melon-colored blossoms dotted a hanging plant; one wall contained a muted rainbow of books. Other than those splashes of color, nothing in the room was of a hue more intense than oatmeal.

Mr Otkin rolled a chair a few feet from Lacey and sat down.

"Before I forget," she began, "my mom said to talk to you about my nightmares. She heard me screaming Tuesday and Friday night. I guess I'm still doing it." Lacey ran her thumbnail along the vinyl armrest, then looked up. "She wants to know when I'm going to get better. I'm supposed to ask you that."

"Dealing with anxiety like yours takes time, and you've only been in therapy three months. If she's concerned, tell her to call me. Now I believe you were talking about Sara. When you had this encounter, did you confront her with your feelings? As you answer be aware of your breathing. That's it – nice and steady."

Lacey blew a cleansing breath between her teeth. Let the energy flow from your fingertips, she commanded herself. "How can I complain when she's helping me? It's like there's this unspoken deal: If she helps me with the work, then I have to listen to the speeches. I really love her, but she lectures me all the time." She sighed and shrugged her shoulders. "I don't know. I guess I shouldn't complain."

Even though she was supposed to shut her eyes, as she spoke Lacey's gaze wandered around the room. Chatting with her eyes closed made her feel weird.

"You say she lectures you. What does she lecture you on?"

"School, mostly. My grades." Suddenly, Lacey drew in a sharp breath. "Oh! You know what she said to me? She's a *lawyer*, and she had the nerve to call me manipulative! Manipulative! Can you believe it!"

"And you disagree with that?"

"No. I am. But just a little bit."

Smiling, Otkin shook his head. "I don't understand. Then what are you upset about?"

"Well, how can she criticize me, when what she does for a living is so *slimy*. Being a lawyer is the ultimate manipulation!"

Mr Otkin leaned forward and let his hands dangle between his knees. A crack of sunlight flashed against his heavy gold wedding band. "Why do you consider it 'slimy'?"

"Because it is! I mean, she puts the scum of the earth back into society, and she gets paid to do it. Don't you think that's slimy?" Lacey felt her whole body tense. Stifling the impulse to chew her lip, she instead cocked her head and flashed a brilliant smile. "Oh, I've got to tell you a joke. This is a good one. Do you know why New Jersey got all the nuclear waste dumps, and California got all the lawyers?"

"No. Why?"

"Because – New Jersey got to choose first!" Lacey's laughter died when she saw Mr Otkin's expressionless face.

Without a word he pushed his chair back to his desk, picked up a leather-bound notebook, then rolled forward again to where Lacey sat. A pair of round, tortoiseshell glasses hung from his neck. Slipping them on, he glanced over her chart. "Lacey, you are a delightful girl, but I'm wondering if you're aware that you tell a joke whenever the conversation wanders into an uncomfortable area."

"I'm a funny person," Lacey snapped. "I like to make people laugh. What's wrong with that?"

"It's not a matter of wrong or right. All I ask is that you become aware of the pattern. Some people . . ." He spread out his fingers in a fanlike motion. "Well, they use jokes as a kind of dodge. They hide behind the punch line. I don't want that to happen to us. The only way I can help you is if you let me explore the areas that are emotionally difficult. For example, we've never resolved the situation with Celeste. She left – how many weeks has it been?"

"Three. She left three weeks ago."

"Hmmm. My senses tell me that a lot of your anxiety is tied up with that situation, probably because you've never settled it. Have you heard from Celeste at all? Has she called, or written, perhaps?"

"No. And I'm glad she hasn't. It's no big thing – we had a fight, she disappeared, then Tamera took her place in the recital. So what's to talk about? Celeste and I weren't married or anything. Friends break up all the time."

"Take a breath, Lacey. You're tensing again. Let's get to the root of this discomfort and discuss the fight. Just let your mind drift back to that day. Think about what happened. What were you feeling? Relax, and let it come back."

Otkin was right. Lacey did recoil when her mind wandered to thoughts of their fight. With Otkin pulling them to the surface, images played through her, like footage on the six o'clock news.

Sitting in the quiet office, she could almost see the frost her breath had made when she'd tramped up Celeste's walkway that day. It had been a cold January afternoon, the kind that felt like dusk even though it was only three o'clock. Celeste had skipped school, probably because her parents were out of town again, so she'd missed the list posted in dance club that day. Lead dancers: Celeste Shephard, Lacey Brighton.

Hopping with excitement, Lacey'd rung the bell, waited, then rung again. She'd listened as the rich chimes echoed throughout the Shephard mansion. "Be home, be home, be home," she pleaded under her breath. She banged the brass door knocker impatiently, then stepped back to examine the front of the house. The upstairs rooms were bathed in light; a shadow flicked across Celeste's bedroom window.

"Celeste!" she'd shouted. "It's me, Lacey! Let me in – I've got something great to tell you!"

She knew how excited Celeste would be when she heard the news. Even though her hands were bare, Lacey packed a snowball and threw it in a perfect arc toward Celeste's window. It smacked against the glass with a loud thud.

"I saw you in there! Open up!" When there was no reply, Lacey sent a second snowball sailing. It landed right on target. Cupping her hands like a megaphone, she'd yelled, "This is the dance police. I will not leave until you report to your front door! *Please come down—*"

The front door banged against the entryway wall. Celeste, clutching a lavender robe to her chest, stood staring. "What do you want?"

When she saw Celeste's face, Lacey's feeling of euphoria vanished. Throwing snowballs suddenly seemed incredibly juvenile. Stuffing her hands into her pockets, she'd walked over to the entryway and stomped the snow from her shoes. "Hi – I – didn't you hear your doorbell?"

"I was taking a bath. What is so bloody important?"

"We got the lead parts," she'd said flatly. "Both of us."

"Fantastic. I'll tell everyone in my neighborhood – I'm sure they're wondering what all the yelling's about."

"Look," Lacey began, "I'm sorry if I caught you at a bad time. I just thought you'd be excited about dance—"

"I am." With a carefully exaggerated motion, she glanced down at her gold watch. "Oh, my gosh, look at the time. My bath has probably turned into ice. I'd better get back inside." She gave a tiny wave of dismissal. "Bye, Lacey. Call first next time."

The door slammed shut. Lacey watched the knocker tap a staccato rhythm against the heavy wooden door. Remembering it now, she knew that it was there, at that exact moment, that she'd made her mistake. Instead of letting it go and walking away, instead of assuming Celeste was in another one of her moods, she'd decided to draw a line in their friendship. No matter what.

Without knocking, Lacey jerked open the door and marched inside. Celeste was already halfway up the spiral staircase.

"What exactly is your problem?" she'd shouted to Celeste's back.

She'd whirled around, her face contorting in a mixture of terror and fury. "You can't just walk into my house! Get *out*!"

"No! Not until you tell me why you're acting like this! What is *wrong* with you?"

"Nothing!" Gripping her satin robe tight, she'd run down the stairs. "You've got to leave. Now."

"No!"

"What?"

"*No!*" Outrage heated Lacey's insides, swelling until her skin felt taut. It was as though her anger hit a flash point.

Celeste had always dictated their friendship, calling Lacey when she was in the mood, walking away when she was not. It was almost as though there were two Celestes: A teenager and a hardened woman who occupied the shell when the young Celeste was gone.

"You know," Lacey cried, "I've always done everything exactly the way you want. Why is that, Celeste? Why do you get to dictate everything we do? And, here's another good question, why do you think it's okay to be so incredibly obnoxious to me?"

Stepping closer, Lacey watched Celeste twist at the fine, braided gold chain she wore around her neck. For once, she seemed nervous.

"You know," Lacey went on, "I've been a pretty good friend to you, and – excuse me for noticing – I don't seem to have a lot of competition for the honor. Get a clue, Celeste. You can't just slam doors in people's faces and expect them to take it. I *won't* take it!"

Celeste had crossed her arms over her chest. Her face cleared; she stared with cool indifference. Now there wasn't even a chink in Celeste's emotional armor. Just icy steel.

"Feel better now?" she'd asked. "My, my, I can tell our therapy is working. You're really beginning to express those emotions. The truth is, you've been shoved at me from the beginning, ever since our mothers started Kaleidoscope Jewels. Think about it, Lacey. I didn't exactly choose you – I inherited you. But that's not a good enough reason to tolerate you any longer."

"Are you saying that you've been faking our friendship?" Lacey had felt the heat of humiliation. It was true – their mothers had pushed them together from the start, but now it sounded as though Celeste had been putting on an act the whole time they'd been together.

"Look," Celeste said, grabbing Lacey's arm and propelling her to the door, "I told you from the start that I like mature people. I don't believe life is just one big joke – I like to *think* occasionally. I mean, going to the mall and stuff is fine, but, face it, you're a flake. And if that hurts you, I'm sorry."

Now, sitting in Otkin's office, she could feel embarrassment stinging inside of her. It was still too hard to think about. Because, even if she didn't admit it to anyone else, she admired Celeste. And that made her criticism burn.

"I'm still not ready to get into that," Lacey said softly. "I know you want me to, but, maybe later."

"That's fine, Lacey. Just remember, you've got to trust me with the hard stuff. I can't help you if you won't let me."

"You're the best friend my mom ever paid for," Lacey told him with a grin.

Otkin didn't laugh.

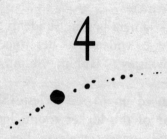

4

"Our locker's a mess, Lace," Tamera complained as she fished for her leotard.

"I know, but it goes with my basic philosophy – a pile for everything and everything in its pile."

Grinning, Lacey shoved a mass of tangled socks and a pair of Keds to the side of her gym locker. "I'm sorry, I'll clean all this junk out later – promise."

"You'd better. Oh, look, there's my *Cosmo* rolled up under your shoes. I haven't even read my horoscope and it's ripped."

"Don't panic!" Lacey grabbed the magazine and said, "Let me see now – I bet if I uncurl this mashed piece and squeeze these two edges together I could read it just fine. What sign are you, anyway?"

"Scorpio."

"Okay – it says here you're unstoppable as long as you care about something, particularly professional achievements."

"Oh, joy," Tamera began. Suddenly she stopped. Her brown eyes widened as her voice dropped to a singsong whisper, "Uhhhh, ohhhh, look who's baaack."

Lacey glanced up to see Celeste Shephard slip into the rear of the locker room. Ignoring them both, Celeste concentrated on her locker combination.

"I thought she quit the recital!"

"So did I," Lacey hissed.

"Then what's she doing here?"

With an exaggerated shrug, Lacey asked, "How should I know?"

Shimmering blond hair framed Celeste's perfect features. Her large, blue-gray eyes were meticulously encircled in kohl, then highlighted with a pale pink that matched her lips exactly. Dark brows arched across flawless skin; fourteen-carat gold swirls hung from her ears like metal smoke. Tall and thin, Celeste was, as always, perfection.

"I wonder what *her* horoscope says?" Tamera snatched the magazine and with a meaningful glance said, "I hope it's something wonderful, like,

'Watch what you eat, the stars predict an explosion of weight in your lower extremities.' Do you remember what her sign is?"

"Celeste? I believe she was born under the dollar sign."

Tamera burst out laughing. Celeste looked over her shoulder, then turned away.

"Did you get the stuff for your costume yet?" Lacey asked as they headed for the gym. She kept her eyes away from Celeste, staring instead at the floor.

"I got my material yesterday. It's a gorgeous blue, sort of like robin's egg but lighter. Do you realize that sometime during the next week I have to learn how to sew? I'm sure you know I am *not* domestic."

As they walked onto the hardwood gymnasium floor, Lacey felt a rush of anxiety. Celeste was back. She'd tried to tell herself that their fight didn't matter, that Celeste had disappeared from her life without leaving a hole, but it wasn't true. She missed her. As difficult a friend as Celeste had been, in a strange way, she'd been worth the pain. As far as Lacey could tell, Celeste had never done anything to please anyone but herself. Sometimes the selfishness drove Lacey crazy, but it gave Celeste an edge. She didn't crave acceptance the way Lacey did. She was strong. Lacey chewed the edge of her lip. She could practically hear

Otkin say, "You're giving in to old stress patterns, Lacey."

Tamera's voice broke into her thoughts. "You know what Crystal told me? She said Celeste went away to a retreat thing for people who have breakdowns. Some ranch in Arizona."

"Really?"

"Marie said if Celeste went there, then she probably met some guy and just partied under the cactus."

Leaning into the cool brick wall, Lacey straightened the strap of her dance suit and tried to look as though nothing was wrong. Stay calm! she told herself. And don't let Celeste see you looking worried – smile!

Their teacher clapped her hands sharply and brought the class to order. Twenty-two girls, members of the Olympus High advanced modern dance team, wandered to the center of the room and dropped into pastel clusters. Lacey and Tamera settled at the fringe of the group. Celeste, poised in a black French-cut dancing suit, stood next to Mrs Giles. Everyone studied them expectantly.

"All right, let's begin. We've got a full schedule. The first item of business is a happy one – Celeste is back!" Mrs Giles squeezed Celeste's arm. "She had to leave us for a while, and I for one was very sorry to see her leave."

"Then you for one are the only one," Lacey

whispered to Tamera. Tamera nodded and rolled her eyes.

"Well, I've got good news. She's agreed to take part in our dance recital. I know I'm bending the rule about missed rehearsals," she continued, as hushed voices rippled from the back of the group to the front, "but she's returned under special circumstances, and I'm thrilled to have her. I've already filled her in on a lot of the dance combinations. So! Let's get started. And again, a reminder – don't forget to pick up your patterns and material after class. We need the costumes completed by Tuesday of next week."

Celeste walked to the back of the group of girls. "She's watching you, Lace," Tamera murmured, elbowing Lacey in the ribs.

"I don't care what she does, as long as she stays away from me."

"All right, ladies, start warming up. We've got *a lot* of polishing to do. While you stretch, I need to speak with Lacey Brighton in my office."

At the sound of her name Lacey froze.

Mrs Giles directed her gaze to where Lacey sat and raised her eyebrows. "Come on," she gestured with a flick of her hand.

Lacey sat, paralyzed.

"Move!" Tamera whispered urgently. "Go on, Lace. Go!"

It seemed to Lacey as though an invisible spotlight hit her from overhead as she followed Mrs Giles into the small, cluttered room. There was no sound or movement from the girls behind her. Just the squeak of Mrs Giles's rubber soles against the floor.

Please, God, Lacey prayed, please, let everything be okay. Please. Please.

"Sit down, Lacey," Mrs Giles said, gesturing to a gray chair. As Lacey dropped into the seat, Mrs Giles leaned against the edge of her desk and folded her arms. She stared a moment before she spoke.

"I've got to tell you right off the bat that you've put me in a very bad position."

"Why? I mean, I know there are things that I haven't gotten down yet, but . . ."

"No, no, don't misunderstand, your work this production has been spectacular. Your dancing, well, your ability is definitely not the problem."

Lacey knit her eyebrows together. "If I'm doing so great, then what's wrong?"

Sighing deeply, Mrs Giles shook her head. "I was ambushed by three of my associates in the teachers' lounge this morning. They're complaining about your work in their classes. I had no idea that you'd let your grades slip so badly – two Ds and a D-minus since I cast you in the program."

Caught. The feelings of being exposed, trapped,

cornered, welled inside her. Fighting the impulse to fire off a nasty barb about teachers and gossip, Lacey forced a smile. She knew she'd have to talk fast.

"You're right, Mrs Giles, I *did* get a little behind, but I swear I'll catch up. The thing is, this quarter's been *the worst*! My other teachers aren't as nice as you are, and the assignments they gave out were *so hard*, and I mean, it's not just me, it's like *everybody's* just dying and—"

Mrs Giles waved her into silence. "I'm sorry, Lacey. You know the rules. It's the policy of the school, not mine. Students who can't keep their grades up simply can't perform in outside activities. I really hate to do this, but I'm afraid I'm going to have to drop you from the show. I've got no choice. I'm sorry."

"That's *not fair*!" Lacey could feel the color rising in her cheeks. Right now, it didn't matter that Mrs Giles was her teacher. What mattered was that everything she'd worked for was disappearing, like a cloud shredded by wind.

"Of course it's fair, Lacey." Mrs Giles folded her arms across her chest. "Mrs Jacobs and Mr Page both told me they'd warned you. More than once."

"But the reason I didn't finish my other assignments was so I could do well in the dance performance! I mean, it's not right to drop me from the thing that made me miss the work in the first place." She looked at her, pleadingly. "And what'll happen to the show? We go on in ten days!"

"Why don't you let me worry about that. I'll figure something out."

"How? I'm the only one . . ." She stopped. A picture of Celeste flashed through her mind. Celeste. Of course. The reason she was sitting there became infuriatingly obvious. "It's not my grades, is it? I'm getting dumped because of Celeste."

"No, that is not the reason. Lower your voice, Lacey."

"Come on – be honest. She's back and wants my part. I mean, she's been *gone* for three weeks while I've been working my buns off, and then she comes back and it's 'So long, Lacey.' Well, forget it! She can't have the part! I've worked too hard."

Now Mrs Giles seemed to blaze. "Celeste has nothing to do with this decision. We're here because of your *grades*. And I'm getting pretty tired of your attitude. You're a *student*. You aren't the one who decides what you will and will not do."

"Is Celeste going to take my part?"

Mrs Giles hesitated. Her eyes darted to the back of the room before finally coming to rest on Lacey's face. "Yes, she's agreed to help us out. It is *totally* beside the point, but she and Tamera will head the performance."

"No, she won't. I swear to you, she won't."

It was quiet as the two of them stared each other down. "Look, I've got a gym full of students out there waiting for me, so we're going to have to finish this up. Until the end of the quarter, you'll spend fifth period in study hall. If you bring your grades up . . ." She reached over and rested her hand on Lacey's forearm. ". . . and I know you can, we'll reevaluate. Okay?"

Lacey jerked her arm from underneath Mrs Giles's polished nails. Her teacher sighed. "Have it your way, Lacey."

"Lace, where are you going? What are you doing? What's going on?" Tamera babbled. She'd been waiting outside the office door, and fell immediately into step beside Lacey. The other girls' eyes followed their every motion. Celeste, on the floor in limber splits, looked up from underneath a raised arm.

"I've been dropped from the program. I've got to spend the rest of the quarter in study hall." It didn't matter who heard. They'd all know soon enough, anyway.

"Oh, *no*! That's terrible!" Tamera's dark eyes widened.

"It's no big deal. I've got to get changed and get my stuff."

"Everybody, take your positions!" Mrs Giles called out. "You, too, Tamera." She clapped her hands, forcing all eyes on her. "And *five, six, seven, eight* . . ."

The blaring music became muffled as the door to the locker room slowly shut behind Lacey.

"Lacey?"

From the sound of the voice, Lacey knew it was Celeste, the one person she didn't want to see. Celeste had won, again.

"I know we aren't really speaking, but I want you to know something. I didn't ask for your part."

"Right, Celeste."

"I swear it!"

"Celeste—"

When Lacey looked up, she saw that there was something different about Celeste. She was thinner, hollow-cheeked, yet she stood erect and determined.

"I realize I'm about the last person you want to talk to right now, but there's something I want to tell you. It's about that day. I'm . . ." She turned so that she faced Lacey. "I'm sorry. I know that's not enough, but there were reasons that I was acting that way. I really am sorry."

"And this is how you show it – by stealing my part?" Lacey asked, jerking her shoe on her foot. "What's next, a knife in the back?"

"No. I know I've done things wrong. I've had . . . problems."

"Who doesn't? You know, this is typical Celeste – everything that happens to you is bigger, or more important, than stuff that happens to the rest of us. I'm sorry, but I don't buy it. Life sucks for everybody."

Celeste's mouth opened; then she clamped her lips firmly shut. "Okay, Lacey, maybe now is not the time. When you aren't so mad, I'd like to talk to you. I realize I haven't always been the nicest person, but what I'm trying to say is that there were reasons."

"Sure, Celeste. Whatever."

"I'll call you."

Lacey didn't answer. She crammed her dance suit into her locker and slammed it shut. Without saying another word, Lacey walked away.

The figure floated through her room, spinning, twirling, a gauzy film covering her face. Closer and closer, the girl danced by Lacey's bed, first on her toes, then landing harder, her movements jerking to a throbbing beat. The gauze shrouded the dancer's face, enveloping her in liquid wings. Lacey strained to see, but couldn't move. A weight crushed her chest, pressing harder, harder, until she felt as though her ribs would split into fragments. Her bedroom door drifted open.

A man stood, eclipsed by a brilliant light. In his hand gleamed a long, silver knife. The dancer spun in fluid circles, oblivious to the figure at the door. Run, hurry, run away! Lacey tried to scream, but her words died in her throat. With a furious movement, the man ripped the gauze from the dancer's face, and as the dancer turned, golden hair arched from her head like a halo. Now Lacey could see who the dancer was. It was Celeste.

The man raised the knife . . .

"No!" Lacey screamed. *Celeste's eyes widened in horror. She lifted her arms as the blade sank into her chest, again and again. Blood etched the gauze like scarlet paint and Celeste crumpled onto the floor. "Lacey," Celeste whispered. "Lacey . . ."*

"*Lacey! Wake up!*" Her mother's urgent voice cut into her nightmare. "That's it, come on. It's just another dream."

The soothing voice guided Lacey through murky sleep.

"You were screaming so hard the dog next door started barking. Wake up, now – come on."

Lacey followed the sound until she broke through to consciousness. Blinking hard, she looked around her room. A shudder passed through her body.

"That was a bad one, wasn't it? Honestly, I don't know why I pay Mr Otkin so much money, when you aren't getting any better."

"You're still dressed, Mom. Did you just get in? What time is it?"

"Two-thirty a.m. With Elaine out of town, I've had to work even later." She pulled off a pair of earrings and sighed. "Between paperwork and our windbag clients, I thought I'd never get home. I'm sorry I leave you alone so much."

"I don't know why I do this. These nightmares . . ."

"It's nerves. You worry too much, sweetie. Things will look much better in the morning. I promise. Now close your eyes and think good thoughts and have a nice dream for a change. That's my girl."

Her mother's nails gently played through Lacey's damp hair. "Go to sleep," she whispered, "that's the way."

Lacey let herself drift into a restful sleep.

"An assembly? I can't believe it!" Sean told her. "This one wasn't posted on our schedule. I always plan my study time around these things. Are you okay, Lace?"

"Sure," Lacey said, swinging her purse onto her shoulder. "Why do you ask?"

"You look really . . . wrung out."

"Thank you."

"No, I mean you're all white and there are dark circles under your eyes."

"Listen, Sean, let me give you some advice. Quit while you're behind."

Sean rubbed the top of his head with his hand and grinned sheepishly. "Okay. I get the message. No more comments on your looks. Except good ones. So right now, I won't say another word."

Lacey stared at him.

"*Oh!* No, that's not to say that I couldn't or wouldn't say something good, if I thought of something – no, that's not what I meant . . ."

"Sean?"

"What?"

"Shut up. Please."

The hallway brimmed with kids heading for the assembly, and from snatches of conversation, Lacey could tell that no one knew why it had been called.

"I wouldn't have killed myself for my physics class if I'd known that I could get extra study time. I've got my book with me, so I can review during the assembly."

"Great."

"I found a really interesting principle. I'll tell you about it inside."

Lacey had to step sideways to weave through the crowd and Sean followed behind, as though attached to her by some invisible leash. It *was* odd to have an assembly called with no explanation, Lacey mused. Olympus High never did anything on impulse.

"Sean, Lace – wait up!" Tamera cried. She waved a notebook over her head like a flag. The three of them settled into their usual seats at the back of the auditorium. A podium stood empty in center stage.

". . . $P = F$ over A. Pressure equals force divided by area. For example, if I hit you with my palm, it doesn't hurt, right? Right, Lace?"

"Right." Sean was on another one of his science kicks, and the best way to handle it was to let him talk. Lacey listened with half an ear as Sean opened his textbook to a chart with a strange-looking graph.

"When my brother used to hit me, it hurt plenty," Tamera offered.

"Did he use his whole palm, or his fist?"

"I don't know . . . his fist, I think."

"See, that's the point. Energy is dispersed across the whole palm if you hit someone like this . . ." He playfully slapped Tamera across the arm. ". . . so there's not much of an impact."

"What a weenie slap. My brother *punched* me."

"That's the scientific principle. If you make your hand into a fist, all the energy is concentrated into a small area. The force is much greater. Or, look here – this shows that a woman in high-heeled shoes can actually puncture the floor of an airplane."

Tamera leaned over and looked at the graph. "You're kidding! How could that happen?"

"Because the weight of her body is concentrated into that tiny area, and then, if you add the acceleration of a plane rising really fast, the point of the heel could drill a hole right through the aisle of the plane."

"Wow!" Tamera said, her eyes wide.

Lacey twisted the bottom of her sweater. She wished Sean wouldn't prattle so much.

"Take a hammer, for instance. If you put it over your head and then smack some poor sucker with it, all the energy from your arm is concentrated into that one-inch area, and . . . splat!"

A chill passed through her as Lacey's mind flashed to her nightmare. She could almost see the blood seeping into the gauze. "Would you stop with the killing already?" Lacey interrupted. "You're making me sick."

"I think it's cool," Tamera said defensively. "I never knew science was so interesting."

"Well, you guys can talk about it later, *alone*. I'm trying to figure out what's goin' on. We've got all the big Olympus High guns up there – Hiatt and Jennings, and I don't know who that is . . ."

The din subsided as Mr Hiatt, their principal, walked to the podium and turned on the microphone. Lifting both arms, he motioned for quiet.

"Students, teachers, I'd like your attention."

A few hoots popped through the auditorium. A paper airplane sailed onto the stage. For once, Hiatt ignored it and instead cleared his throat, hugging the maple-colored wood as though it were a life raft. "As you know, we at Olympus High

have a close-knit student body," he began. "There's
. . . there's a unity here."

As he spoke, his gaze wandered back and forth
across the large auditorium. "We are a family.
What happens to one of us does, in effect, happen
to us all."

"Typical Hiatt," Lacey whispered. "He never
could get to the point!"

Sean put his hand on her arm. "Quiet! Something's happening!"

"All of us at Olympus, from the teachers down
to those who keep this facility clean, have a deep
love for each and every one of you students. As
part of our commitment, we try to keep the
ugliness of the world at bay. But sometimes the
world insists on dragging its violence into our
home. Into our family." Mr Hiatt looked at the
teachers standing at his side, and then straight into
the center of the student body. "I don't want you
to learn of this tragedy through television or gossip.
So it is with deep and profound sadness that I
inform you of the death of one of our own. Early
this morning, Celeste Shephard was found murdered in her home."

Waves of "Oh, my God!" and "I had a class
with her" rushed through the auditorium. Lacey
sat, stunned. It wasn't possible. It simply wasn't
possible. She had spoken with Celeste yesterday,
had dreamed of her in the dark hours of the

morning. It was impossible that Celeste would just cease to exist. A life didn't extinguish without warning, a soul didn't just leave its body and float away. Not like that. Not by murder.

Tamera began to cry, her shoulders shaking silently, and Sean looked as though he were locked into a rigid grid. But Lacey felt nothing. There was nothing to feel, because there had been a mistake. There was no way Celeste could be dead. Period.

A middle-aged woman in a dove-colored suit stepped up to the microphone and waited for the din to subside. The sound of a girl crying was muffled as she buried her head into the shoulder of a stoic boy.

"My name is Helen Ewer, and I will be available to any of you who would like to talk to me. Death is always a shock, especially if it is a violent one. I want you to know that my associates and I are here for you. If any of you would like to talk about this, please come in. We'll be stationed at the main office and also at the library. Please, feel free to lean on us."

"Excuse me, I have one quick thing to add." A short, thick man stepped up to the mike. "I am Detective Yandell, and I want to say that if any of you has had recent contact with Celeste, I'd like to speak with you. I'll be here at the school all day today. Thank you."

"This assembly is now over. Those of you who

wish to talk to a counselor, you're excused from class. The rest of you . . ." Mr Hiatt seemed to choke, then said, "I'm sorry. God bless you."

Sean reached over and hugged Lacey as the lights of the auditorium blazed on.

6

A stack of books dug into Lacey's thighs. Restless, she flipped open the top volume and tried for the hundredth time to read, but the words were meaningless. Nothing could penetrate the chill that kept her from understanding. Cold. That was how she felt. Her blood had turned to ice, and scattered thoughts froze like crystals on a windowpane.

Mrs Thomas, the librarian, tiptoed over to where Lacey and eleven other students sat waiting for their turn with the counselor. They formed a stoic line along the library wall, moving up one chair whenever a red-eyed student left the inner office. It seemed as though they played some sort of strange childhood game – wait, move up, wait, move up – until the one at the head of the line finally stood and took her turn in the librarian's office.

"I'm going to leave for just a minute," Mrs Thomas said in a low voice. "I know this is hard, but will you all please respect the other students studying in the library and remain quiet?"

Everyone nodded.

"All right then. If Mrs Ewer asks for me, tell her I'm in the auditorium." As the library door drifted shut, a girl next to Lacey laid her head against the wall and stared at the ceiling. When she opened her mouth to speak, Lacey noticed she had neon braces.

"Well, at least the warden's gone."

A boy with bristly blond hair let out a snicker. Lacey opened her book again and tried to read, but the girl turned toward Lacey and extended her hand. "Hi, I'm Alicia. You knew Celeste, didn't you?"

"Yes," Lacey murmured.

"I didn't. I mean, not very well. She was in my math class, but she didn't talk much. My teacher said I didn't actually have to know her to come in here for counseling, because the whole thing is so traumatic. Was she nice?"

Lacey shot a look that she hoped would make Alicia's mouth freeze, but Alicia didn't seem to notice. "I bet you're glad you're next," she went on, shifting in her seat. "You've been sitting here longer than I have, and I think my buns've turned to wood." The girl spoke in an easy, conversational tone, as if shared tragedy somehow made them friends. When Lacey didn't answer, she sighed and ran her fingers through short, dark hair. "I really hate to wait, don't you?"

"I guess."

"The whole thing is so – gross. I was wondering, 'cause you knew her, have you – have you heard any . . . details?"

Lacey felt herself stiffen. Her fingers pressed between the pages of her book and gripped the smooth paper.

"I've heard a couple of things," a girl three from the end offered.

"Really?" Alicia asked. She turned from Lacey to the girl. "You know, what I'm really scared of is that the killer is still out there! I mean, maybe he'll come after me!"

"Oh, I wouldn't worry – I bet he'll only take a blond."

The guy that had snickered looked interested. "How come?"

"My uncle's a policeman, and he says that these crazies have a pattern. Like, it might be that this guy'll just kill blonds, or maybe his thing is long hair. Just watch, I bet the next one he gets will look just like Celeste."

Lacey watched as the line transformed itself into

a semicircle. It was as though they were sharks drawn by the smell of blood, instead of friends grieving the death of one of their own. Disgusted, Lacey turned away. She wouldn't listen to their whispers, but their voices nibbled at the edge of her mind.

"You know how Celeste's dad is a diplomat? Well, they think that somebody came to get the dad, and when he found out that only Celeste was home, he killed her instead. It's like supposed to be a political message."

"I heard they found her in her bedroom, and her hands were tied behind her back with a rope."

"I heard that, too! Did you hear the thing about her panty hose?"

"No!"

"Sandy said she heard she was strangled with her own panty hose."

"That is so sick! Just imagine how bad it must have been – some guy choking you and right then you *knew* you were going to die!"

Lacey glared until their whispers died. Were these people supposed to be her friends, Lacey wondered? She didn't recognize any of them. Celeste had always maintained the kids at Olympus were socially retarded.

"The guys all act like little boys," Celeste had told her, "and the girls pass notes the same way they did in junior high. You're the only one I can really talk to."

Before attending Olympus, Celeste had always gone to private schools. Her parents had decided their daughter needed "mainstreaming," but the Shephards' experiment hadn't worked. In the half year that Celeste had been at Olympus, she'd stayed at the edges. She'd made neither friends nor enemies, but passed through the school as if it were punishment and her only option was to serve the time.

Lacey pictured Celeste's perfect eyes. Had she seen her killer? Had she turned around and seen him standing in her home? Had she had time to scream . . . *Stop!* Lacey felt herself jerk in her seat. Don't think about it! The glass windows of the office were enshrouded by curtains that had been pulled shut. Lacey prayed the boy ahead of her would hurry.

The door opened quietly and a boy shuffled out. This was it. Lacey gathered her books together and stood.

"Good luck!" the girl with the braces called out. She gave Lacey the thumbs-up sign.

With the curtains closed, the office seemed more like a cave than a room. A box of Kleenex sat on the edge of the desk. A kind-looking woman stood and extended her hand.

"I'm Helen Ewer, and you're . . ."

"Lacey. Lacey Brighton."

"Lacey. What a lovely name. Have a seat, Lacey, and I'll tell you a little about myself. First of all, I'd really like you to call me Helen. Is that all right with you?"

Lacey nodded.

"Good. I'm a counselor that the board of education has contacted because something catastrophic has happened, and what I try and do is walk people through the pain so that they can deal with it. I really hope that I can be of some help to you." She reached over and squeezed Lacey's hand. Her fingernails were unpolished and ragged at the edges, as though they'd been bitten. From a distance she'd seemed pretty, but up close her looks were flawed. Tiny red veins spread like thin roots around the edges of her nostrils, and fine, dark hair shadowed her upper lip. Even her suit looked rumpled.

"I have two children, I have a private practice at the university, and I'm very glad you felt comfortable enough to come in here and talk with me. I have to tell you how wonderful it is to see so many young people reach out for help, because the wounds heal much more quickly when you share the pain. Now then, you know a little bit about me, so why don't you tell me about you. Are you a senior?"

"Yes."

"Could you spell your last name for me? And tell me how you knew Celeste."

As Lacey spelled her name, Helen scrawled some words on a piece of paper. "It's okay if I take a few notes so I won't forget anything, isn't it?" Helen asked, looking up.

"I guess."

"Great. Go on then, please. How did you know Celeste?"

"We – we were in the same dance class. And we were best friends."

"Oh. I'm sorry. That must make it especially hard for you."

A wave of pain crashed against her, but Lacey took a deep breath and went on. "I have a counselor that I go to, Mr Otkin—"

"Yes, I know him." Helen smiled. "He's good."

"—and he says I worry too much about things I can't change. The thing is—" A ragged breath escaped from Lacey. "The thing is – Celeste and I were best friends, but not for the last month. We were – we were in – a – fight." Her throat seemed to close against the words, but she swallowed and forced herself to go on. "I keep thinking about how I can't go back and change things. Celeste is dead, and I can never make it up to her. I can't go back and fix things."

"No one ever can," Helen said gently. "But, Lacey, people argue all the time. You can't have imagined that something like this would happen, and I'm sure, with enough time, you and Celeste would have worked out your problems. Celeste knew that."

Balling her hands into fists, Lacey drilled them into her cheeks and tried to force herself not to cry. It was strange, she'd been able to maintain in the auditorium, had held on in the library, but now, her insides churned like the waves in a storm. "I saw her yesterday. I watched her tie her shoes. I can't get that picture out of my mind . . . her fingers, and her stupid shoes . . ." Lacey felt a Kleenex being shoved into her hand.

"That's okay, let it out, Lacey."

"I can't – it's *hard*!"

"It's okay. Let it out."

"You know what the worst – part – is? I had a nightmare – last night. I dreamed a man stabbed her over and over, and there was blood everywhere, and she fell down and just stared at me and called out, 'Lacey . . . Lacey.' And now – she's – *dead*!"

"You dreamed Celeste was murdered?"

"Yes!"

"You dreamed a man stabbed her – you dreamed this last night?"

Sobs raked through Lacey, hot tears blinded her eyes. "There was blood, and a man, and, oh, God, I just went b – back – to sleep!" Lacey's head pounded to the beat of her heart; and yet, it felt good to let some of the pain wash out of her.

"That's really strange – about the dream. Here, take a Kleenex, that's it, dry your eyes, good girl. Now, take a deep breath, and tell me what you saw."

"Why? It was just a nightmare."

Helen tapped her pen against the paper. She looked as though she were deciding whether or not to speak. Finally she said, "Look, Lacey, this may sound very strange to you, but I need to ask something very important. Did you see the man's face? In your dream – could you tell what the man looked like?"

"No. I don't know. Maybe."

"Visualize it. Try to picture exactly what the man said. What he did."

"Why? I don't want to. What difference does it make what I dreamed?"

"Because, the fact is, Celeste was stabbed. Many times. And you dreamed she was stabbed. That connection is probably just a coincidence, but there is an outside chance that last night you had some sort of psychic experience. And if you did, then you saw the face of a killer."

7

"So, you must be Lacey. I'm Eric Yandell, and from what Helen says, you and I need to talk."

Detective Yandell pulled a chair next to Lacey and dropped into it. He smelled like aftershave, only not the rich-smelling kind that Celeste's dad wore. Yandell's fragrance was a cross between lemons and disinfectant soap. Salt-and-pepper hair curled on his head, and when he spoke his dark, close-set eyes examined her intently.

"I wish you and I were meeting under better circumstances," he said, grasping her hand in a firm handshake.

"Me, too." Pulling free, she hunched her shoulders and gripped her elbows hard.

There was a silence.

Ever since Helen had called Detective Yandell, and had left Lacey sitting alone in the librarian's office so she could speak to him in private, Lacey'd had a sinking feeling in the pit of her stomach. It was the same feeling she'd had when she was seven, and spilled a bag of marbles down Cannon Hill. As the brilliantly colored glass ricocheted in a hundred directions, she'd run, panting, squatting to the asphalt, desperately trying to snatch them up. But she couldn't. They'd gotten away from her.

"Detective Yandell was very interested in your dream," Helen prompted. "Why don't you tell him what you told me?"

"I don't know, it's hard. I don't like to keep thinking about it." Lacey directed her words to the floor. "Besides, it was only a bad dream."

Detective Yandell smiled encouragingly. "You're right, Lacey, and it probably means absolutely nothing. But right now I have a dead girl and no clues, and I need to hear what you've got."

"Why? I'm not a psychic or anything."

"No one is saying you are," Helen broke in. "Our position . . ." She looked at Yandell and added, "The position of the police department – is to leave no stone unturned. It used to be people laughed at things like dreams and psychic energy, but not anymore. Besides . . ." She rested a hand on Lacey's shoulder. "What could it hurt?"

"I understand all you've been through," Detective Yandell went on. "And I'm sure this is very painful. The intriguing part is . . ." His eyes made a sweep around the room, and his voice dropped low. "What I'm going to tell you can't go any farther – understand?"

Lacey nodded.

"I'm talking about friends, your father, your mother – I don't want you to breathe this to anyone."

"I promise, I won't say anything."

He moved even closer, so that there was almost no space between them. Helen hovered breathlessly behind them. "All right then. Some of the details of your dream, well, they are very similar to what actually happened to Celeste."

A tremor passed through Lacey.

"There isn't a lot of evidence at the murder scene. It's early yet, but, to be honest, we need all the help we can get. Will you tell me what you saw?"

Sweat gathered at the edges of her hair; she wound her fingers into knots. It seemed so surreal – these two adults, waiting eagerly for her to tell them details of a night terror. No one seemed to care that she had come for help. Now it was she who was supposed to give it. But what if they were right, and she could help them catch the dark man in her dream?

"Relax," Helen told her. "Take in a deep breath."

For once it felt right to Lacey to close her eyes. She pressed her fingertips into her forehead; Helen's hand smoothed the top of her hair.

"Start from the beginning," Yandell said gently. He pushed a button. "I'm going to turn on this tape recorder, just so that I don't miss anything you say." He paused. "Is that all right with you?"

The image of the marbles ricocheting down the hill flashed through Lacey's mind. "Yes, it's okay."

Yandell's voice was soothing, calm. "You said you were lying down. Was it in a couch or a bed?"

"A – a bed. I think it was my bed. I saw a girl, Celeste."

"What was she doing?" Yandell asked.

"Dancing. She was dancing, twirling, with some floaty blue material all around her. At first I didn't know who she was, but then the material slid from her face. I knew it was Celeste."

"In your dream, did Celeste see you?"

"No. It was like I wasn't there at all. She kept dancing, and I was watching her. And then—" Lacey drew in a sharp breath.

"It's okay, Lacey," Helen whispered. "Keep going. You can do it."

"And then – there was a man. He was standing by the door, watching her."

"Can you tell where the door was? Was it the living room door? Can you visualize that?"

Squeezing her eyes tighter, Lacey strained to see into her mind, tried to bring the dark images to the surface. "I think – it looks – like the living room door. Her living room door. I – can't be sure."

"That's fine, Lacey. What else do you see?"

"The man is coming closer – I want him to stop, but he doesn't. He has a knife, and he raises it. I try to warn her, but I can't. He lifts it over her and—" A sob exploded from Lacey. "There was this weight, like a heavy weight, on my chest. I tried to scream, but I couldn't! And the man – he came up behind her and he raised his arm and he stabbed her again, and again, and again! There was blood! Everywhere, there was blood!"

"Could you see the man's face? Try, Lacey. Try to see it."

"No! It's too dark. I can't tell."

The image of the man slicing Celeste with the blade cut into her mind. "Twelve – no – thirteen times. I think he stabbed her thirteen times!"

"Where? Where did he stab her?"

"In the chest – on her back – once across her neck – I don't know! It's too hard! I don't want to do this!"

"Try!" Yandell commanded. "Tell me what you see!"

"Celeste is falling. She's crumpling up on the floor!"

"Where is the man?"

"He's gone. He – it's like he disappeared."

"What is happening to Celeste? Where is she now?"

"She's on the floor."

"Is she alive?"

Lacey swallowed, hard. "I think she is – yes! She's still alive. I remember – she said my name, over and over, and the blood made a pattern on the rug, then she looked up at me . . ." Lacey's eyes flew open. Yandell looked strained, as if the dream shook some deep, inside part of him. His notepad lay limp on his lap; he clutched his pen tightly.

"There's no more," Lacey said, her voice shaking. "I'm sorry – that's all I remember. I – I woke up right after that."

Yandell leaned over and clicked off the recorder. "You did fine, Lacey. Thank you."

Helen gave him a tiny nod, her lips pursed into an expression that seemed to say "I-told-you-this-was-strange-now-do-you-believe-me?"

"Can you use any of this? Is her dream helpful at all?" Helen asked him.

Rubbing his hand over his chin, Yandell shook his head softly. "I'm not certain."

"Surely you must have some opinion!"

"I'm not free to discuss the details of the case

with either one of you. All I can say is, I have no idea what's going on here. In all my days on the force, I have never believed in that mumbo-jumbo stuff. Fortune-tellers laying their hands on pictures of victims, then wasting everybody's time driving around to God-knows-where so they can bilk money out of some desperate sucker." He took a breath, then blew it slowly between his teeth. "But there are parts of this dream that make me think I might have been wrong. The number of stab wounds, the blue material, the location of the crime, even the laceration across her neck . . . Lacey, I will tell you that what you saw is close. Damn close. Maybe there is more to this world than just the things we can see and touch."

"What happens now?" Helen asked him.

"I'll talk to the medical examiner and the guys in forensics. Then I'll play them the tape. I want them all to hear this."

Her insides shaking like a rabbit, Lacey asked, "And then what?"

"I'll let you know."

8

The paintings were beautiful. A small child dressed in burgundy clung to a scarlet swing; three huge valentines hovered against the wall. As Lacey glided along the museum hallway, she smelled red roses blooming in the centre of a canvas. "Do you like this one?" a shadow asked her. As she moved closer, rose petals dripped from the painting onto the floor. A breeze began to stir; the petals drifted around her feet like autumn leaves. "Look what you've done! Pick them up!" the shadow commanded. Lacey gathered armfuls of petals, but they became liquid, bleeding through her arms, her fingers, seeping into her dress. A light blazed behind the shadow; she couldn't see anything but the inky black at the center of the flame. "You know who I am. Look at me. You know who I am . . ."

* * *

"Wake up, sweetheart, I'm here."

As Lacey swam to consciousness, she realized she was still on the living room couch, sprawled across her mother's lap. With an even, rhythmic motion, her mother had been stroking Lacey's back, and the movement seemed to mark time with her waking thought; Celeste is dead. Celeste is dead.

"You had another bad dream, didn't you? You were making little crying sounds."

"Is . . . is Celeste gone?"

Her mother nodded.

Lacey blinked and pulled herself to a sitting position. "How long have I been asleep?"

"About an hour. You were dreaming so hard, I didn't want to wake you."

Her mother had come home early, and Lacey had let herself collapse into her arms. She'd cried, talked, cried some more, then melted into an exhausted sleep.

"Are you hungry?" her mother asked gently. "I could make you some toast."

"No."

"You're going to have to eat sometime. How about a cup of tea?"

"I don't want anything."

"All right, if you're sure." Sighing, her mother raked her fingers through her hair. "I just wish Sara weren't out of town right now. You know, I have to call Elaine, but, my God, what can I possibly say to her? Things like this are impossible to comprehend."

"I – I want to send the Shephards flowers, to their house I mean, not just for the funeral. Celeste likes," Lacey swallowed, then went on, "liked, anything lavender."

"I think that would be nice."

Her mother stretched, then bent to rub the circulation back into her legs. With her mother's head angled that way, Lacey could see a faint growth of silvery roots.

"You know, Lacey, while you were sleeping, my mind kept going over all of the things that you said. I'd like to talk to you about this psychic business. Why don't you come sit with me while I make myself a bowl of hot soup. I have the urge to do something – normal."

"You go on. I'll be there in a minute."

As her mother disappeared into the kitchen, Lacey felt emotion gash her insides like broken glass. Images of Celeste flashed through her mind: Celeste's thin hands punctuating the air as she made a point; Celeste smoothing her hair behind her ear as she read a book. Celeste sitting apart from the others in dance class, head down, hugging her knees tightly to her chest. Lacey could almost hear her laughter.

"This potato is bad," Celeste had said to Lacey

after she'd plucked it from her tray and sniffed it. She'd wrinkled her face in disgust.

Lacey had grabbed the potato, studied it, then given it a good healthy smack. "Bad potato. Bad, bad, bad!" Grinning, she'd handed it back to Celeste. "I don't think it will give you any more trouble. The secret is to be firm with these spuds." Celeste had thrown back her head and laughed, and Lacey had noticed how straight and white her teeth were.

"You're crazy, Lacey," she said. "You're the only person who can still do this to me. It must be wonderful being you. Nothing in your life is serious, it's all just material for another joke."

Don't think about it – don't think about her! Lacey commanded herself now. She shook her head. First the dreams, now these images. It seemed as though Celeste possessed her mind.

The microwave beeped.

"Come on, honey, soup's done," her mother called out.

Lacey rolled off the couch and headed for the kitchen. Since the divorce, her mother had rewritten every part of her life, including her decorating style. Their old home had been like an indoor garden, with soft, pastel flowers on the furniture and potted birch trees filling up the corners. But their new home was pure Danish modern. Clean, sharp lines defined every room. Except for Picasso reprints framed in black lacquer, the walls were completely bare. In the kitchen, bleached oak cabinets had been accented with plain brass; square enamel pots held miniature cactus; and the curtains had been replaced with bronzed window blinds. Their whole house had an edge.

"Come on," her mother said, patting a bar stool. "Sit."

Lacey slid onto the seat and rested her elbows on the countertop.

Her mother placed a bowl in front of her. "I know, I know, you're not hungry, but you can at least breathe in the steam. Chicken soup vapors are healthy."

"Thanks."

"Are you feeling any better?"

"Not really. My eyes feel all puffy and my head hurts. I can't stop thinking about, you know . . . everything."

Her mother sat down beside her and placed an old black-and-white photograph between them. Lacey tucked her feet on the bottom rungs and waited. Whatever her mother was about to say seemed to make her nervous.

"That's my Grandmother Abby. She's your great-grandmother."

The woman in the photograph had her hair pulled into a severe knot. Leather high-top boots were brushed by the hem of a dark skirt, and although she wasn't smiling, her face seemed gentle.

"I recognize her picture."

"Of course you do." Her mother cleared her throat. "I've never mentioned this before, because, well, frankly, it's always seemed rather silly. But this thing with your dreams has got me thinking." She touched the edge of the photograph, then looked at Lacey. "When I was a little girl, my mother told me stories about my Grandma Abby. Family legend says she dreamed an arrow pierced a huge ship. In her dream, the boat tipped over and sank, and hundreds and hundreds of people drowned. The dream was so real to her that she told everyone about it. Two months later a ship named the *Lusitania* was attacked by the Germans. It was torpedoed. No one survived."

Lacey's heart skipped a beat. "Really?"

"Of course, the family interpreted that to mean my grandmother had seen the future. I've never actually accepted any of it, but my mother was a believer."

"What else did your Grandma Abby see? Did she ever dream that somebody was murdered, and then have it come true?"

"I don't think so, but I can't say for certain. My mother always threatened to write these stories down, but she died without leaving so much as a page."

"Don't you remember anything?"

Narrowing her eyes, her mother looked off into the corner of the room. "The only other anecdote I recall was the one about my Great-Uncle Albert. During World War One, my grandmother dreamed her brother Albert was shot. He was serving in France at the time. Three days later a telegram arrived saying he'd been wounded. He got it in the leg, I think. Anyway, the point is that the family worked out the times, and they swear that she dreamed her dream at the exact time Uncle Albert was hit."

"That's amazing!" Lacey breathed.

"Maybe. I was never that impressed. I always felt that if a man was fighting in a war, the chances of him taking a bullet were rather high." She paused, then shook her head. "But now, I've got to consider you and your nightmares. And this connection with Celeste. It's possible that Grandma Abby did have some kind of power and it skipped a couple of generations."

Lacey chewed the bottom of her lip. "Detective Yandell told me that he couldn't explain my dream. He said that if my nightmare checks out, it could be the key to solving the whole case. He even talked about reinterviewing me under hypnosis—"

"Wait a minute! He wants to put you under hypnosis? Why?"

"Well, Helen Ewer – she's the counselor I told

you about – said hypnosis might help me see the face of the killer. She even suggested that Otkin do it. She says he does hypnosis, and she thought he would be a really good choice because I already know him."

Her mother seemed to hesitate. "I suppose if it were Mr Otkin, that would be acceptable, but I do not like people making plans for you without asking me first. Maybe other people don't understand the tremendous stress this has put on you, but I do."

"Don't worry, I'll be okay. I told them I'd do anything I could to help," Lacey said softly. "Anything."

The chiming of the doorbell broke the silence.

"I'll get it. You just sit and try to eat." Her mother hopped off her stool, then turned and patted Lacey's hand. "Listen, I want you to remember one thing. Just because someone is dead, well, that doesn't automatically turn them into a saint. Celeste was a wonderful person, but she was difficult. She was lucky to have had you for a friend."

"It doesn't feel that way, Mom. But thanks for saying it."

Moments later, there was a rumble of a man's voice at the door. Lacey couldn't make out the words, but she could tell her mother was protesting something. Finally, she appeared at the kitchen door. Detective Yandell walked behind her.

"Honey, there's a detective here to see you. He says it's about Celeste."

"Hello, Lacey," Yandell began. "I'm sorry to bother you, but the report from the coroner just came in."

A stubble of beard shadowed his face, and his clothes, so neatly pressed that morning, now seemed tired and rumpled. He looked directly at Lacey and shook his head. "It seems the details of your dream were quite accurate. We'd like to explore your dream as parapsychological evidence."

Lacey swallowed, hard. "What happens next?"

"First of all, I want to tell you that you don't have to do this. But if you want to," he said, then glanced at her mother, "and if it's all right with your mom, we'll pick you up tomorrow and put you under hypnosis. I really want you to try to focus on the man's face, and I think we need to put you under to get at those details. Mr Otkin has already agreed to help. Will you do it?"

Almost imperceptibly, her mother nodded.

"Okay," Lacey answered.

"Wonderful!" Pushing up his glasses, he rubbed his face, then squinted. "I've got to tell you, after reading that report – well, you've made a believer out of me. We're going to try and take you back into your nightmare, Lacey. If it works, I think we're going to nail the person who murdered your friend. You've got my word on it."

9

Lacey barely heard the doorbell over the blaring of the television set. She didn't move. She'd spent the last two days wrapped in a down-filled comforter, wedged into a recliner that had been shoved directly in front of the TV. Her mother was at work, so that meant Lacey had the entire house to herself. Sipping a Diet Pepsi, she let herself be pulled along by an episode of "The Brady Bunch." On the show, Mike and Carol Brady wrung their hands anxiously, in the hopes that their son Bobby would win an ice-cream eating contest. "Go!" the television master-of-ceremonies shouted.

It was Thursday. Celeste had been dead for three days, and Lacey had hidden herself in the den, trying to deafen the voice inside her that screamed nonstop. Celeste is gone, Lacey, and you can never go back and tell her you're sorry for walking out on her when she tried to make up. You'll never ever know what she wanted to say. It's too late. You'll never get another chance. Celeste is dead. You walked away. It's too late.

Stop it! Lacey commanded herself. Pulling the comforter tightly under her chin, she rooted for Bobby as he devoured swirls of whipping cream and chocolate. She didn't want to think, or even feel. Just be absorbed into the world of vintage comedies. Think about Bobby and the ice cream, and you won't hear the voice.

A small square of light reflected in the corner of the television screen. A shadow passed through it, like the winking of an eye. It took her an instant to understand that there was someone else in the room. Every muscle in her body became instantly taut; she felt the presence behind her, could hear soft breath sounds. A hand rested lightly on her shoulder.

"Hi, Lacey."

"*Gawd!*" Lacey exploded. "You scared me to death! Sean, what are you doing here?"

"This is for you," he said, setting a potted fern on a table nearby. "I know how bad you must feel. I wanted you to know that I'm here to help."

Flakes of snow had melted in his hair, beading like a string of clear pearls. The cuffs of his jeans and his sneakers were wet; he smelled damp and earthy.

Lacey raked her fingers through unbrushed hair and tried to pull herself together. "The door was locked," she protested. "How did you get in here?"

"Magic! Hi – it's me," Tamera quipped, stepping into view. "I made Sean go in first in case you shot him or something. Your door *was* locked, but he worked some weird stuff with his library card and it opened right up. Can I turn this off?" she asked, pointing to the television set.

"I don't care."

Tamera flipped off the set. With a meaningful glance at Sean, she said, "He *swore* you wouldn't get mad if we broke into your house. Look at her face, Sean. You were wrong."

"I'm not mad, just spooked."

"He goes, 'She's not answering the phone, she won't come to the door, let's go in and get her!' Are you sure you're okay?"

"I'm fine. I've just been vegging out on Pepsi and TV. I haven't even brushed my teeth – I must look like a mess. It's just, I couldn't face going to school right now, and my mom said it was okay if I took the week off."

Tamera patted the top of Lacey's head, then leaned over and hugged her hard. "Hang in there, Lace," she whispered. "It's going to be okay." When she stood, her voice resumed its usual bounce. "Oh, I wanted you to know that the fern's from me, too. Except I wanted to give you roses. *Big* mistake, going in with Sean. He just had to get you this bizarre plant. It curls up when you touch it."

"It's a mimosa," Sean said defensively. He set the plant in her hands. "Roses die, but if you treat it right, the mimosa can outlive us all. Its name means 'fake sleep.'"

As Lacey turned it, the fine, spider-thin branches seemed to shudder at the movement.

"It responds to touch," he explained. "Just put the tip of your finger on its edge, and then see what happens."

"I don't know . . ."

"It won't hurt you. Just try it."

Reluctantly, Lacey brushed the end of the fern with her index finger. The branch closed together, like two hands folding in prayer. She touched another; the fern recoiled, closing in on itself. That's just the way I feel, Lacey thought. Absently, she stroked branch after branch, until the plant looked as though it were dead.

In a low voice, Tamera murmured, "I *told* you we should have gone with roses!"

"No, no, this is great. Thanks, you guys." Lacey set the plant back on the table. She looked at them, and tried to force a smile. "Listen, I know you've both tried to get hold of me, and I haven't called either one of you back. Sorry. I'm just dealing with a lot of stuff right now."

"I've been talking to your answering machine since Tuesday, and it's Thursday already," Sean complained. He dropped to the floor and kicked off his shoes. "I did get ahold of your mom, though. She told me about the psychic stuff and the hypnosis. What's going on?"

"I don't know. It's been really strange. But before I get into that, no one has told me when the funeral is. Do you know? I mean, I haven't seen it in the paper and Mrs Shephard hasn't called."

Tamera sank beside him and stared at Lacey. Static crackled as she pulled off her coat, creating a halo of jogging-suit fuzz that looked like a blue aura.

"They announced it at school. The funeral is this Saturday," Tamera said softly. "I thought the three of us could go together."

"Oh. That would be great."

"It's taking five days to bury her because they had to keep her body an extra long time at the coroner's. The medical examiner needed to check it for—" Sean stopped abruptly. Lacey wasn't sure, but she thought she saw Tamera kick his ankle.

Tamera quickly changed the subject. "So, your mom said you went under hypnosis at the police station. Why didn't you call us? Weren't you scared?"

"It wasn't so bad."

"But weren't you afraid of letting someone else take over your mind? Like, what if the hypnosis guy told you to go rob a bank, and you did it 'cause he commanded you to and you were caught and thrown in jail—"

"That's not reality," Sean broke in. "Can I have some of those?" He eyed a half-empty can of Pringles potato chips. When Lacey nodded, he went on, "Anyway, hypnosis doesn't *make* you do anything. You won't commit an act that you wouldn't normally do. It's just a tool to help you get into your subconscious mind." He crunched a handful of chips and licked his fingers. "The dream is what I wanted to ask you about. Your mom honestly seems to believe that you had a psychic experience."

"And you don't?" Lacey flared. It was just like Sean to question something he couldn't explain. The tone in his voice was his I-don't-believe-it-prove-it's-true style. "You know, it wasn't just me or my mom that thinks I'm psychic, it's the police, too! They wouldn't waste their time this way if they didn't believe in me! They told me they got some real solid leads from my dream."

"Don't get me wrong. I'm just calculating the pure odds of you having a bad dream at the same time something catastrophic happened. Consider the fact that you've been having nightmares for months now. I'd say the chances of this happening are pretty high."

Coolly, Lacey asked, "So what's your point, Sean?"

"My point is that this whole thing is probably just a coincidence. Which means the police have put you through a whole lot of crap for nothing."

"Except, I saw things that really happened. I saw blue material, and I can tell Detective Yandell thinks that's important. Plus, in my dream Celeste was stabbed, just the way the real killer stabbed her. How do you explain that?"

"I bet she's a psychic," Tamera broke in nervously. "Anyway, you still haven't told me what the hypnosis was like. Is it like on TV? I mean, did they use a watch on the end of a chain and swing it back and forth or something?"

Sean groaned. Lacey pulled the comforter into a ball and hugged it to her stomach. "No," she said, giving Sean a look, "it was just me and Otkin sitting in a room. I don't remember much – just him talking to me real soft, and counting backward, and then I was out."

Narrowing her eyes, Tamera said, "Do you remember what you said?"

"Nope. It's kinda like dreaming. And I think it was a break having someone I know doing the hypnosis. Otkin helped me a lot, so that I wasn't so nervous or anything. They're going to call me if they need anything more." She spoke directly to Tamera. "I'm glad they think my dream can help. It makes it . . . easier."

Propping himself on an elbow, Sean grinned wickedly. "So, what now? Palm reading? Tarot cards? Maybe we should get you a crystal ball and call you Madame Lacey."

This time Lacey was sure. Tamera kicked Sean. "Sean," Tamera said, "shut up."

At that moment, the doorbell chimed. Lacey looked at Tamera and Sean with dismay. "Now what?" she wailed. "I can't believe this! I bet it's Sara – she's been out of town and she's due in this afternoon. A hundred bucks says she rags on me for never calling her back." Sara had left at least six messages, but Lacey hadn't wanted to face the kind of questions Sara was sure to ask. Sara always rooted around, trying to dig into her mind. Why couldn't people just leave her alone? "I know!" Lacey said, snapping her fingers. "One of you guys go answer the door and tell Sara the answering machine was accidentally dropped into the bathtub. Tell her I lost the number where she was staying, and that's why I couldn't call her back, and it's not my fault those machines glitch out under water."

"Stop! This is too good to waste," Tamera said lightly. "You just sit there and perfect your excuses, and I'll get the door."

Once Tamera left the room, Sean rolled to his feet. For an instant he said nothing, just looked at her with his intense, dark eyes. He leaned forward and gave Lacey a soft kiss. He tasted good.

"I'm really sorry you've had to go through this. I might not show it, but I know this has been hell for you. And I've missed you."

"I've missed you, too."

He touched the tip of her nose with his finger. "It seems like I see a lot more of Tamera than I do of you. I don't like that. Makes me think terrible, dark thoughts."

"Yeah? Like what?"

Sean kissed her again. This was the magnetism that kept Lacey from moving on. It was the way his lashes curled, so thick they brushed his brows, and his peppermint breath, and the way he got excited about stupid plants. His hovering could make her insane, but Lacey could bank on the way Sean really cared for her. More than any other guy she'd ever known.

"You still haven't told me about your dark thoughts," she murmured, pressing her forehead into his. For the first time since the murder, the knot in her stomach loosened. Maybe hiding from people wasn't the way to get over the pain. Maybe her mother was right. She shouldn't run from those who loved her.

From the doorway to the den, Tamera cried,

"There are two policemen here to see you, Lacey. They say it's important."

Sean jumped back. "Policemen? Why?"

"Wait! Did you tell them I was in my pajamas?"

"I did, but they said it didn't matter."

"But—"

Pushing past Tamera, two policemen marched into the room. They stopped in front of Lacey.

"Are you Lacey Brighton?" the older officer asked brusquely.

"Yes. I – I feel dumb about not being dressed. Is this about the dream?"

A young officer clutched a paper in his hand. He glanced at it, then stared at Lacey.

"This is a warrant for your arrest. You, Lacey Brighton, are being charged with the murder of Celeste Shephard." While the other officer began to read Lacey her rights, he leaned close, so close that she could smell the coffee on his breath. "I think you'd better call a lawyer."

10

The noises of the other inmates rumbled through the jail. Metal doors came together with an ominous clang; women's voices altered pitch like notes on a wooden flute – some high and thin. Others were discordant moans. Lacey lay on her cot, away from the other prisoners who had gathered around a television soap opera. She tried to piece together the bits of her life, shattered twenty-four hours ago. The shards came together in an ugly collage.

Within minutes of her arrest, she'd been hand-cuffed and driven to jail. A stern policewoman had taken her into a room and patted her down.

"You don't need to do that – I don't have a gun," Lacey had protested.

"Procedure," was the terse reply.

The policewoman led her to a table where a male officer had directed her to sit in a nearby chair. Sergeant Kirkis, she'd quickly read from his badge.

"Your watch, and your ring, too, have to be removed and put in this bag," he'd told her.

Lacey's skin had been so cold that the ring had slipped easily off her finger. Hands trembling, she set it on the Formica tabletop.

"Mr Kirkis, I shouldn't be here – there's been a mistake. My friend, Celeste, was killed, and I had a dream, and – I didn't—"

"Yes, ma'am. We're going to have to check in all of your property, including everything in your handbag. After we're done here, you'll need to change your clothes and be fingerprinted and photographed. After that, you can make a call. Understand? Now, will you take your purse and empty it for me?"

"But I didn't do anything!" Tears had stung her eyes, yet he'd looked at her without expression.

In a calm, empty voice, he'd ordered, "Please, ma'am. Empty it."

Reluctantly, Lacey had turned over her shoulder bag. Keys, a brush, a wallet, and a half-eaten roll of Life Savers scattered across the table. Strangers, people she had never met, were going through her things, touching them – touching *her*, and in the process were handling her soul. She had become as helpless as a little child. And there was nothing she could do.

"Lip balm, strawberry," Kirkis had muttered. "Keys, three on a brass ring." As he methodically itemized the contents of her purse on a mimeographed sheet, Lacey had tried to control the panic that welled inside her. It's a dream, she'd repeated again and again. An officer marched past, escorting a drunk man to a nearby cell.

"Room Five-sixteen," the officer had called into a walkie-talkie. The door clicked open, and the two of them walked inside.

A policewoman appeared, leading a slouching, hard-looking girl. Bleached, frayed hair hung in the girl's eyes, like the fringe on an old couch. The girl had stared at Lacey, pulling back her lips in an eerie grin. As they walked by, she'd leaned toward Lacey and hissed, "See you inside."

Fluorescent lights glared off the walls. There were no windows, just a labyrinth of walls and officers and bars and metal slamming into metal. "I'm in another nightmare," Lacey had whispered to herself. "I'm going to wake up."

"Excuse me, did you say something?"

The sound of Kirkis's voice had made her jump. She'd quickly shook her head no and hugged her arms to her chest.

"Your sister is Sara Brighton, right?" He must

not have seen her nod. "Sara Brighton," he'd repeated, this time more slowly. "She's your sister?"

"Yes. Is she here? Can I see her?"

"No, but I can tell you that she's already put a call through. You're lucky to have someone on the inside pulling for you. If everything comes together, you could be out of here by tomorrow. Just stay loose until then, okay?"

She'd been led through a maze of doors, fingerprinted, photographed, had been ordered to shower, and then, the worst humiliation, been sprayed for lice. A dingy gray sports bra, underwear, and a jumpsuit had been handed to her by a willowy woman with deep brown eyes.

"This should be your size. I'll supply you with a cup and a toothbrush. Everything I give you will be counted and accounted for. I've assigned you a cot at the front of the cell, so no one should bother you there. Do you understand everything I've said?"

Lacey had nodded her head yes. If I do everything exactly the way they tell me to, they'll see I'm a good person and let me go, she'd told herself.

And now, as she lay on her cot, she knew that as long as she lived she would never forget the sound of the bars crashing shut. And the eyes of the other women in the cell. No matter what happened now, she'd already been to hell.

* * *

"Brighton, Lacey," a crisp voice demanded, "you're wanted in the visitor center. Your mother and sister are here."

As she pulled herself off the cot and smoothed her orange jumpsuit, she could feel the other women stare. She made her way to the door of the cell and waited for the bars to be opened.

"Stay beside me," the stocky policewoman barked. Lacey followed her into the corridor. From the corner of her eye, she could see the limp hands of inmates dangling between bars.

"That's the one who wasted her friend," someone yelled.

"Whoa, girl, your butt's gonna fry."

"Tell 'em you didn't do it, baby. That's what we all say. Tell 'em you don't know nothin'."

Lacey stared straight ahead, focusing on the thick, bullet-filled belt the policewoman wore. Like a rat in a maze, she moved precisely where she was directed.

"In here," the guard told her. "Just pick up the phone and talk."

Lacey stepped into a small, tired-looking room. A table stretched across one wall, and above it were telephones separated one from another by panels of wood. Through a rectangle of glass, Lacey saw Sara and her mother, who gave her a forced smile and a wave.

"You've got thirty minutes," the guard told her.

"The door will lock behind you. I'll be back right on time."

Lacey slid onto a wooden chair and picked up the receiver. Her mother did the same.

"Are you okay?" her mother asked shakily. "Has anyone hurt you?"

"No. I'm all right. But I want to get out of here. Please! I want to go home!"

"Don't worry, sweetheart. Your father is putting up bail—"

"Daddy?" Lacey's stomach squeezed. "Does he know?"

"Of course – I had to tell him. He's mortgaging his house to get you out of here. But we'll talk about that later. Sara has managed to get your arraignment set for this afternoon, which is marvelous. If she hadn't gotten your case heard so quickly, you would have been held the entire weekend."

"Fridays are usually booked, but I pulled a few strings," Sara said.

"So – so keep your chin up. I – I love you."

"I love you, too, Mom."

Lacey could hardly recognize her mother; the Claret Red, Olivine, and Rosewood makeup were gone; dark circles shadowed her eyes, and her skin was ashen. Sara leaned close to the receiver, so she, too, could hear what was said.

"You look really tired. Are you okay, Mom?" Lacey asked.

Her mother nodded, but looked quickly away. Her shoulders shook softly. With one hand she pulled a tissue from her purse, pressed it into her eyes, and took a deep, wavering breath. "I'm sorry, honey. I promised your sister I wouldn't do this. It's just, seeing you in this horrible place, with all of these criminals . . ."

"It's not that bad – everyone's left me alone. That's the bright side." She smiled. "The other inmates are afraid to mess with a killer."

At that Sara jerked the receiver away. "My God, do you have the faintest idea of how much trouble you're in?" she exploded. "Do you realize what kind of mess you have gotten yourself into? What you did was so stupid! Thinking you were psychic! Why did you say *anything* to the police? Their business is to take words and make a noose out of them."

"I was trying to help."

"Your nobility is about to be repaid big-time – you're being charged as an adult. With *murder*!"

Pulling the receiver close, her mother said softly, "I want you to listen to your sister. She's been working nonstop since she heard what happened. I don't think she's slept a minute."

"I'm not allowed to represent a family member," Sara interrupted. "It's a conflict of interest. We *do* have options, though. Here, Mom, hold the phone." She opened a briefcase, and pulled out a leather-bound tablet of paper. She took back the receiver and cradled it in her shoulder. "I want to hire a private attorney. In fact, I've already made inquiries to see who can take you fast. Cohen is razor sharp, and Washington knows his way through every loophole there is. I'd like to make the final decision."

"You choose whoever you want," Lacey said, trying to keep her voice steady. "Just make sure he knows I'm innocent. I know everything will be okay because I didn't do it. All I want is to talk to a judge. The judge will see how ridiculously stupid this whole thing is and then I know I'll go home."

Shaking her head, Sara said, "Oh, Lacey."

"What? You get guilty people off all the time, Sara. There's no way I'm going to prison when I didn't commit a crime. Innocent people don't go to jail. It doesn't work that way!"

"Look at me, Lace. And listen." Sara pressed a palm against the glass. Her eyes narrowed, but this time, Lacey saw a glint of something that made her blood chill. It was fear. Sara, who played the law as if it were a board game, was scared.

"You are in the system now. You're being charged with murder. Remember your report? I told you then that this isn't about 'fair'. This is about winning. And the other side has a tight case already lined up against you. They're saying that there is no way you could have known what you did about Celeste's murder unless you committed the crime. Celeste was working on her dance costume when she was killed. Her blood was all over the blue material, just like you said it was. Her throat was cut, just like you told them. You want to know what the prosecution will do? They're going to get a psychiatrist who will testify that your dream was a confession. They're going to contend that you couldn't admit what you did through your conscious mind, so you confessed through your dreams. I know the way they operate, Lacey. Quit fooling yourself with 'fair'. This is real."

"No! *No!* Why are you trying to scare me?"

"Because I have to. I need you to use every ounce of your intelligence, and work with me. You can't screw around with this, Lace. The stakes are too high. The DA is going after you as an adult, and he's charging you with special circumstances. Our state has the death penalty. That means if you lose . . ." Sara began to falter. "If you lose . . . my God, Lacey . . ."

Sara didn't have to finish her sentence. Her face said it all.

11

"Slip your hands into these cuffs. Tell me if I get them too tight," Officer Swenson said.

With her wrists cuffed to a thick leather belt, Lacey could hear her heart pound in her ears, like the rapid, terrified beating of a bird's wings.

"Where am I going?"

"To your arraignment. It's time."

A small, middle-aged woman with too much makeup, Officer Swenson placed her hand under Lacey's elbow and led her down a hallway.

"Here," she said, pointing to an elevator. She punched the down button. When the door slid open, Lacey saw that the back half of the elevator was barred.

"Open elevator cell," Swenson called into her

walkie-talkie. After a buzz and a click, the lock on the bars released.

"In there." She motioned Lacey into the cell. Pulling the bars shut, she turned and pressed a button marked BASEMENT.

"This elevator will take us to a tunnel that runs from the jail all the way to the courthouse. Are you claustrophobic?"

"No."

"Fine." Officer Swenson's hair had been dyed to an otherworldly orange. Rolled in tight curls and heavily sprayed, it moved with her head like a helmet.

"I understand you got Cohen to be your lawyer," she said, stabbing her hair with a cherry-red fingernail. "That right?"

"My sister said she'd try to get him. Is he good?"

"He's slime."

Lacey's stomach squeezed. "Excuse me – what did you say?"

"I said," Swenson growled, "he's slime. Scum. He takes murderers from our jail and puts them back with the decent folks, and then they just kill again. Real nice. You must be awfully rich or awfully guilty to need him."

"No – that's wrong. I'm not rich, and I didn't do anything—"

Officer Swenson snorted.

"I am *not* a killer!" Heat rose to Lacey's cheeks.

Metal bit her wrists as she strained against the cuffs, but Swenson calmly turned away and stared at the elevator doors.

"I remember now, you're a psychic. Okay, Ms Brighton, tell me, what am I thinking right now?"

"It doesn't work that way!"

"Umm-hmmm."

"Wait a minute – you don't know me!" Lacey screeched to the back of Swenson's head. "How can you assume that I murdered someone? Because I was arrested? What ever happened to 'innocent until proven guilty'? I'm *innocent*!"

"Oh, come on. Save it." The elevator bumped as it hit the bottom, and once again, Swenson barked, "Open elevator cell," into the walkie-talkie. *Buzz*, then *click*, and Swenson motioned Lacey out. Stepping aside, she waited until Lacey moved in front of her.

This is the way it's going to be, Lacey thought. Strangers have already made up their minds. The truth doesn't matter; nothing matters. A weight spread over her, until it seemed as if her every breath was heavy, labored. I can't stand this. I can't stand this. I won't stand this.

"You going to court, Betsy?" a guard asked Swenson. He eyed Lacey up and down, and then dismissed her. Almost as if she didn't exist.

"I'm due there in ten minutes, so you need to open up the wormhole. I swear, I could give up my aerobics if I just went through this thing every day."

The guard chuckled. He pressed a button, and a set of bars groaned ajar.

"See you on the trip back," he told her.

"You bet."

It was cool in the tunnel. The rounded walls were made of cement, yet they had a faint greenish cast from the rows of fluorescent tubes that lined the ceiling. Their shadows moved ahead of them in dark fractures. The air smelled different. Used. Overhead camera lenses followed them as they walked. Because the passage curved, Lacey couldn't see more than twenty feet ahead. Every sound echoed; their footsteps, the whine of the cameras, the heavy jingle of Swenson's keys. The tunnel seemed endless.

"Here we are," Swenson announced. Another elevator glided up seven floors. It opened to a small dingy room with an uncovered toilet in one corner.

"This is the holding cell. Your lawyer will meet you in here shortly, and then you'll go before the judge. Sit on the bench and wait."

Lacey stepped into the small room, hardly bigger than a closet. She was only two feet inside when the elevator doors slipped together. Swenson left without uttering a word.

She was alone. She paced the room, staring into the rusty toilet bowl. The heater grate had metal bars bolted over it. Everything was locked or barred or bolted. How long had it been since Swenson left her there? Minutes? It seemed like hours.

She dropped to the bench, reading the graffiti that had been scratched into its dull paint. There was a knock, and the sound of a key in the lock. An athletic man with dark, thinning hair entered the room. He walked over to where she sat.

"Lacey, I'm Barry Cohen. I'm a lawyer, and I've agreed to take your case. It's a pleasure to meet you. Please call me Barry."

He shook her hand, even though it was still cuffed to her belt. His suit was an expensive gray, and the burgundy swirls in his tie exactly matched a folded pocket square. He spoke quickly, and his movements were brisk, intense.

"Don't worry," he told her, eyeing the belt, "that will come off before we get into court. I want you to know that I've seen your sister and she sends her love. Now, the first thing I want to tell you is not to panic. If things go the way I expect them to, you'll get out of here in just a few hours. How does that sound?"

"Like a miracle."

"I wish we would have had time to get you your regular clothes, but, as you know, this has been a rush. No matter, orange is very becoming to you." He smiled, then set his briefcase next to her and snapped it open. As he shuffled through papers, he muttered, "You know, you never should have been charged as an adult. They did what's called a direct file . . ." Glancing over, he cried, "Hey, are you okay? You look like you're going to faint."

"I'm, I . . ."

He shoved his briefcase aside and sat beside her. "You've got to stay with me, Lacey. Come on, think tough. I need you in there."

"You haven't even asked, and I want you to know." Tears dripped onto her jumpsuit. "I did *not* kill Celeste. I didn't do it. I swear to God!"

"I believe you, Lacey. I've read through the report, I've talked to your sister. They went after you because it was easy. As far as I'm concerned, there are two victims here. Celeste, and you."

Great, heaving sobs wrenched her. She was embarrassed because she'd held so much in for the twenty-eight hours since her arrest, and now she'd unleashed a torrent of emotion.

"Why are they doing this? Why? I – can't – believe – this is happening to me."

"Hold on, let me wipe your eyes. It's hard to cry with cuffs on, huh? You can't even blow your nose." He took out a clean handkerchief, and gently rubbed the tears from her cheeks.

"I'm sorry," Lacey wept. "I don't know what's wrong with me."

"You're scared to death, that's what's wrong. But you're going to have to pull yourself together.

This arraignment is very important, and I want your head up high. No tears. Can you do that?"

Lacey nodded. She took a deep, wavering breath. "What's going to happen now?"

"Any minute we'll leave here and go to court. You'll appear before Judge Aaron Campbell."

"Do you know him? Is he nice?"

"*Nice* isn't a word I'd use. He's old school, but he's fair. Make sure whenever you speak to him that you address him as 'Your Honor.' He'll review the charges, and then ask you how you plead."

"Not guilty. I'm *not guilty*!"

"You tell him that. I already believe you."

"Please state your full name for the court," Judge Campbell commanded.

Trying to keep her voice steady, she replied, "Lacey Amelia Brighton."

"Is this your attorney?"

She glanced at Barry, who stood with her behind a podium positioned directly in front of the judge.

"Yes, Your Honor."

Judge Campbell opened a file and glanced through it. His thick, white hair made a dramatic contrast with his black robe. His skin was leathered, and his knuckles seemed too large for his hands. But when he looked at her, his eyes seemed kind.

"Lacey Amelia Brighton, you have been charged

with the capital offense of homicide in the first degree, of section ten-three-four of the state penal code. It is charged that you did willfully and wantonly assault Celeste Shephard on February eighteen of this year, stabbing her about the torso and neck until she was dead. How do you plead to these charges?"

"I didn't do it, Your Honor. I plead not guilty."

"The court accepts your plea. I hereby order a preliminary hearing to be set for thirty days from this date."

"Your Honor," Barry cried, clutching the podium, "bail was set at two hundred and fifty thousand dollars. I feel my client should never have even been charged as an adult, and request that you take her age, which is only seventeen, into consideration in deciding the issue of bail. A quarter of a million dollars is a ridiculous amount to ask in this case." He held up his fingers, touching them as he spoke. "First point, my client has no prior history of a crime of any kind. Her record is completely clean. Second, her family is part of this community – she is hardly a flight risk. And third, Ms Brighton must attend her senior year at Olympus High School, where she is a vibrant and model student. Bail this extreme will be difficult if not impossible for her to attain."

"Your Honor, Ms Brighton is a cold-blooded killer."

A chunky, well-dressed woman stood and walked toward the bench. Barry leaned close and whispered, "That's Kathy Brewer, prosecuting attorney."

"The State will prove that Ms Brighton is an unstable woman already under psychiatric care," Kathy continued. "There is evidence that this crime was planned well in advance. We have testimony that Ms Brighton was furious when she lost her part in a dance recital to Ms Shephard. When told of her suspension, she did in fact warn her teacher, Mrs Giles—" Kathy glanced at a paper. "This is Ms Brighton speaking now, Your Honor. Quote, 'I won't lose this part. I swear to you, I won't.' Unquote. We will prove that it was this jealousy that caused her to murder her one-time friend."

"That's not true!" Lacey exploded. Barry gripped her arm and shook his head.

"She went to the victim's house and viciously stabbed Celeste Shephard fourteen times." Walking close to Judge Campbell, her voice became hard. "Fourteen times. Three of the wounds were sufficient to end Ms Shephard's life, but the stabbing went on and on and on. Your Honor, this was more than murder. It was overkill. And for that reason, I'm asking that bail remain at two hundred and fifty thousand dollars. Thank you."

Judge Campbell leaned back in his chair. He stared at Lacey, then down at her file. With a quick movement, he closed her folder and set his hands on top of it.

"I am always uneasy when dealing with someone as young as you, Ms Brighton, but age cannot be a factor in my decision. You were charged as an adult when the warrant was issued; your age is no longer relevant."

He laced his fingers together so that they formed a bridge. He looked at Kathy Brewer. "This is a very brutal crime. Although I feel that Ms Brighton is not a flight risk, I am persuaded that she could be a threat to the community. Therefore" – he picked up his gavel – "bail is to remain at two hundred and fifty thousand dollars. Court is adjourned."

The bang of the gavel was like a bullet in her soul.

12

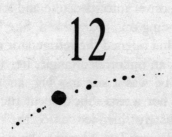

"Hello, is Tamera there?"
   "Who is this?"
Lacey felt her stomach clench. "It's Lacey. Hi,
Mrs Belmondi."

"You're out of jail?"

"Yes. I got home last night. Is Tamera there?"

"Just a minute." There was a pause. Lacey heard
a muffled, "It's Lacey Brighton. I can't believe it
– they let her out." After a moment, Tamera's
mother said crisply, "I'm back. What do you want
Tamera for?"

"I need to talk to her about the funeral. Is she
there?"

"*Celeste's* funeral?"

"Yes. It's this afternoon. She and I were going to go—"

"I don't think so. Good-bye, Lacey. Please don't call again."

The dial tone droned in Lacey's ear. She replaced the receiver into its cradle and stared at it.

"What's going on?" Sara asked. She walked into the kitchen and opened the refrigerator door. Sara's hair hung in an uncombed tangle; her yellow terry cloth bathrobe was a size too big, and the sleeves hung below her wrists. She'd spent the night, and had immediately blended into their home as though she'd never left. Shoving the sleeves up her arms, Sara opened the crisper drawer and pulled out an apple. "Who were you talking to?"

"I just tried to call Tamera. Her mother won't let me speak to her."

"Witch!" Sara spat. "Don't let it get to you. Lord, it is so unfair the way people jump to believe the worst. I'm sorry, Lace. I'm sure Tamera doesn't feel that way. You want anything to eat?"

"No, thanks. Prison food ruined my stomach."

"I'll bet." Sara padded over and slipped onto a stool beside her.

The east side of the kitchen was glass, and the February sun poured through, heating the room until it almost felt like summer. The Saturday paper lay unopened on the counter. Celeste's obituary was inside, but Lacey didn't want to see it. Not yet. She needed to pretend her life was normal for just a little while. With her own home, her sister, and the sun-warmed kitchen, she could almost imagine her life was the way it used to be. Even though it never would be the same again.

"Where's Mom?" Sara asked.

"She's gone on a doughnut run. Dad called while you were in the shower. He said to give you a hug."

"Did you know he had to raise twenty-five thousand dollars for your bail? That really put the squeeze on him. It's lucky you only have to fork over ten percent instead of the whole amount." Sara took a bite of apple. "I don't know anyone who could afford the whole two hundred and fifty thousand."

Cringing, Lacey moaned, "Don't say that, okay? I already feel horrible. At least when I'm found innocent, he'll get his money back. Right?"

Sara shook her head no.

Lacey's eyes widened. "You mean he'll lose *all* of the twenty-five thousand? Even though I didn't do it? That's not fair! Dad can't kiss off twenty-five thousand dollars! I can't let him – I should go back to jail!"

"No, no, no. He was happy to help you. I just want you to realize how much he cares. He'll fly out when your trial begins, and he told me he'd do whatever it takes. He really loves you."

Pushing her eyebrows with her fingertips, Lacey cried, "I can't believe he put his house up for my bail. I wonder what Angie thinks?"

Sara snorted. "I'm sorry, but the words *Angie* and *think* can't possibly go together. Wait a minute," she said, rubbing Lacey's back. "I saw a smile. You actually grinned, just the tiniest bit. There's hope."

In a voice barely above a whisper, Lacey said, "When I was in jail, I thought there wasn't any hope. I thought I'd never ever smile again."

Sara reached over and pulled her close. Thick terry cloth muffled the small, internal noise of her sister; the soft sound of Sara's breathing, the steady beat of her heart. It had been years since Lacey'd had a hug like that from Sara. It felt good.

"Everything's going to be okay," Sara whispered. "I promise."

"You can't make guarantees like that," Lacey murmured, clutching her sister harder. "Before I told Yandell about my dream, I remembered the time I spilled all those marbles down Cannon Hill. Now I think I know why I flashed on that."

"Why? I don't understand."

"It's because, once I said those words, I couldn't get them back. They got away from me, just like the marbles did." She looked up into Sara's eyes. "Does that make any sense?"

"Yes, it makes perfect sense." Sara stroked the

top of her head. "You know, words are pretty tricky things. I've been thinking a lot about them myself. When I saw you in jail, talking to me through glass, I said to myself, 'If I were the DA, I could make a case against her. And I could argue the case so well that they'd put her away. And it would be wrong. I would be wrong.'"

"I'm glad you're on my side."

"The thing is, I've never given much thought to the people I take apart in court. It's pretty scary to realize that the law is more than just a game. It's lives."

"When I told them about my nightmare, I didn't know it could get so far away from me. It seems weird to think that telling a dream could hurt me like this."

"It makes me sick, the way those officers manipulated you," Sara growled. "They played you for a sucker, Lace. The psychic thing was pure flattery. They told you that you had powers, and you rolled over and talked."

"You don't think my dream was real?"

"Who knows?" Sara shrugged and straightened. Lacey could tell their "moment" was over. "Maybe you picked up some of Celeste's mental energy, maybe not. I guess if you forced me, I'd have to say I think it was pure coincidence."

"That's exactly what Sean said."

"The point is, I don't think a jury is going to

believe that you're a psychic. The prosecutor's going to have ten psychiatrists testifying that you were giving the police a veiled confession. They'll hammer away at the odds of your dream and the murder scene matching up. It's the biggest problem you're going to face."

"I can't deal with that now," Lacey groaned. "I don't even want to think about it. Inside, I already feel so . . . dark. This day is going to be the worst day of my life."

"I'll ask you one more time – is there any way I can change your mind about going to Celeste's funeral?"

Lacey shook her head no.

"Do you want me to come with you? I think it's a terrible idea, but I'll help you in any way I can."

"Thanks, but you really didn't know Celeste. And anyway, Sean's going to pick me up. I want a chance to see my friends. I want them to know that I . . . that I . . ."

"I understand. Just be careful, Lace."

"The funeral doesn't start for half an hour," Sean said. "Are you sure you want to go in?"

"I'm sure. It's freezing out here, and I . . . I need time."

"Whatever you want, Lace. I'm here for you."

Flowers of every kind filled Saint Peter and

Paul's Cathedral. The waxy smoke of candles, the sweet heavy scent of roses, the bitter pungency of chrysanthemum all mingled to make a kind of incense, which wafted through the warm air. Even though it was dim inside, the stained-glass windows rainbowed brilliant color. Organ music played from somewhere overhead, and the notes almost covered the quiet sound of mourning.

"I think we should sit in the back," Sean whispered.

The two of them took off their coats, then slid into an age-darkened pew. The church was only half-filled, and everyone else had taken a place in the front. Lacey pressed against a large pillar. It felt cold against her skin.

"Her casket's by the altar," Sean said quietly. "It's closed. I'm glad they didn't have a viewing."

"I don't know if I can look. I really don't think I can."

"Hold my hand, Lace. It'll be okay."

Slowly, Lacey felt herself being drawn forward. She wanted to see, and yet felt repelled by the reality of the coffin and what lay inside. A huge crucifix hung in the center of the altar. Her eyes drifted from Christ's anguished face, to his pierced feet, and beneath to Celeste's coffin. The casket was a dull silver. White roses had been piled on its top in a delicate mound; football chrysanthemums and lavender carnations filled vases at either end, and behind, a cascade of blossoms curved in a floral wall.

"Oh, God," Lacey cried softly.

"It's okay, Lace."

"All of a sudden, it seems so real. I knew she was dead, but it's like, I didn't . . . I can't breathe."

Sean pulled her close. He looked pained, as though he wanted to help but didn't know what to do. All he managed was a soft, "I'm sorry. I'm really, really sorry." After a moment, he said, "Look, there's Tamera. She's with Crystal and Marie. I'm going up to let them know we're here."

He hurried down a side aisle. Even though they'd been dating for months, Lacey had never before seen him in a suit. As he wove through the pews to where Tamera sat, Sean seemed to disappear into a sea of other dark-suited men. It's like a uniform, Lacey thought. The color of this day is black.

She watched as Sean placed his hand lightly on Tamera's shoulder. He leaned close, pointing to where Lacey sat. Tamera turned toward her; her eyes narrowed. She stared at Lacey, then at Sean, all the while shaking her head from side to side. Gesturing stiffly, Sean looked both grim and intent. Crystal put her arm around Tamera and shot Lacey a withering look, while Marie hugged her arms closely to her sides.

Sean walked back alone.

Notes from the organ pounded to match the beat of Lacey's heart. What was it they were playing? "Amazing Grace"? Sean kept his eyes down, unconsciously walking in rhythm. He slipped into his seat. Absently, he picked up a hymnal, then replaced it in its holder.

"They – Tamera said she wanted to stay up front."

"She won't come, will she?"

Sean stared at his hands. "No."

"Marie? Crystal?"

He shook his head.

"Oh," Lacey managed to say. "Okay, then."

More people filed by. Men and women, all in somber colors, moved quietly, deliberately. Was it her imagination, or did their eyes slide over her as they walked past? She shrank against the pillar, but it seemed as though she couldn't hide from their stony glances, or the hiss of their whispers. She clenched her fists so tightly that her fingernails bit into the palms of her hands.

"Excuse me, I'm Bernard Shephard. May I have a word with you two?" Whirling around in her seat, Lacey saw a tall, thin man with razor-sharp features. He looked like Celeste's father, only older.

"You're Lacey, aren't you? And you must be Sean."

Trembling, Lacey whispered, "Yes, that's right."

"As I said, I'd like to speak with you. Could we do this outside?" Bernard asked, pointing to a side door. "Please."

Lacey began to get up, but Sean pressed his hand against her knee, holding her in place. "Why?" Sean demanded.

"I'd rather discuss this somewhere else."

"I'd rather not."

Bernard's features hardened. "Very well, then. This is difficult. I'm Celeste's uncle, and on behalf of the Shephard family, I'm respectfully asking you to leave this church. They don't want you here. No one does. Your presence, Miss Brighton, is in very poor taste."

Lacey's insides reeled. Why hadn't she listened to Sara? Somehow, she'd convinced herself that her friends wouldn't believe the lies, that the Shephards would be glad to see her, that the funeral would be a comfort. Like dust in the wind, her illusions blew away. She took one last look at the rose-covered coffin. Maybe Celeste is the lucky one, she thought. Clutching her purse, she rose to leave.

"Lace, we don't have to go," Sean said icily. "It's a church, for God's sake."

Bernard focused his gaze on Sean. "And you, Sean, aren't welcome, either. I realize you and Celeste were friendly, but you made a mistake in the end. I don't believe I need to make myself more plain."

Lacey watched Sean color, then pale. Bernard's eyes looked as hard as flint. "I would like to escort you both through the back way. Let's be as discreet as possible. Get your coats."

Sean gathered up their things. Without a word, they left the warmth of the cathedral and entered the February cold.

13

"Those jerks!" Sara cried. "They actually had the nerve to throw you out of a church? I'd like to sue them all, including that twit Tamera! What a vicious little turncoat—"

"It's my own fault. You tried to tell me," Lacey said, straining to keep her voice steady. "I should have stayed home."

Sara draped her arm around her sister. Her overnight bag was packed; it lay crumpled against the front door. She'd been ready to walk out when Lacey had arrived, but had stayed planted in the doorway until she'd heard everything that happened.

The unkempt version of Sara seemed to have been folded away alongside her yellow terry cloth robe. Now her hair was smoothed to a perfect sheen. A thick silver chain and matching earrings shone like streaks of lightning against her navy-blue turtleneck. As Sara pulled Lacey close, the smell of lingering cigarette smoke drifted up from her clothes, but Lacey didn't care. She needed the hug.

"It seems like years ago when I came to your courtroom to do a report on the law," Lacey murmured into Sara's shoulder. "I don't even feel like the same person anymore."

"I don't think I do, either."

"Remember when I said our legal system was the best in the world, but only if you're guilty?"

Sara stroked her hair. "I remember."

"When I said that, I really believed it. I watched you get Earl Craw off, and everything about the trial seemed like such a joke." Lacey pulled back so she could look her sister right in the eye. "I thought, 'He's guilty. He did it, or he wouldn't be sitting there in court. Sara's got no right,' I thought, 'to get this criminal off.' But now that I'm on the other side, now that I'm the one accused, it's all so different! 'Innocent until proven guilty' – that's what the law says. That's what is right. I'm supposed to be innocent until proven guilty."

"Sweetheart, you are! People know that."

"That's a joke. Everyone, *everyone* treats me like I murdered Celeste, even before I've had a trial. When I was sitting in that church, I could just feel people hating me. At first it really hurt; now, it just makes me mad as hell."

"Good," Sara told her. She squeezed her tighter. "Come in here and sit down." Leading her by the hand, Sara pulled Lacey into the living room. The back of their salmon-colored sofa was covered with a layer of square pillows. As Lacey sat down, she pulled a pillow to her stomach. Sara sat beside her.

"You know what I'd like you to do, Lace? Hold on to that anger, and use it. Remember that game we used to play when we were little, the one where scissors cut paper, and rock breaks scissors?"

Lacey nodded. On car trips, the two of them played round after round for what seemed hours.

"The way you feel now works something like that game." Sara made a fist with one hand, then laid her flattened palm over the top of it. "Remember how paper covers rock? Well, anger covers hurt. I'd rather see fire in your eyes than that awful hound-dog look. Let yourself be mad. Go kick a few walls, and then go find Tamera and kick her, too."

Lacey gave a half smile and looked at her feet. "I'll put on a pair of my pointiest shoes."

"Perfect. Aim high. You know what? With all of this heavy talking, I really need a smoke." A leather purse dangled from Sara's shoulder and rested on the sofa. Snapping it open, she rummaged through its contents, but instead of a cigarette she produced a Baggie full of carrot sticks. She looked at Lacey sheepishly. "However, rather than smoking, I will eat a nutritious carrot. Aren't you proud?"

"What – you're quitting?"

"Trying to. I have to admit, veggies don't give me quite the kick, but you've been pleading for me to stop and I figured now was a good time. Want one?"

"Thanks." Lacey plucked a warm carrot from the Baggie and looked at Sara in amazement. Sara, quitting smoking? In the past, every time Lacey had produced an article about the hazards of nicotine, Sara had countered with, "You're my little sister. I tell you what to do, not the other way around." But like everything else in her life, her relationship with Sara was changing. There'd been a subtle shift in the way they were connecting. Now Sara was listening to her, and defending her with a ferocity more intense than any she'd ever used in court. Sara wasn't talking at her, she was talking to her. Lacey realized that she and Sara were finally becoming equals. No, Lacey thought, it's more than that. We're becoming friends.

Glancing at her watch, Sara's eyes widened. "Oh, sweetie, I've really got to run. The office called, and even though it's a Saturday, I have to go in."

"That's okay. All I want to do right now is soak in a hot bubble bath. Go ahead, I'll be fine."

"Before I leave, I want you to think about something. There is a quick way out of this mess."

"How?"

Sara took a bite of carrot, and pointed what was left of it at Lacey. "You didn't kill Celeste, but somebody did. If the real murderer is caught, you'll be off the hook. It could be that simple."

Pulling on a cuticle, Lacey asked, "What about my nightmare?"

"Forget it. At least for now, let's deal with reality. Someone killed Celeste. That's a fact. And whoever did it is still free."

Lacey hugged the pillow hard. She'd been so consumed with her dreams, with being accused of murder, that she'd not really thought about the obvious. It was like looking through a camera at a scene up close, only to have the lens pulled suddenly back. A murderer was out there, breathing, thinking, waiting. The police weren't looking for him. And he – or she – knew it.

Softly, she asked, "Where do you start looking? I mean, who could have done something like this?"

"At this point, it could be anybody. It could be a stranger. It could be a crazy." Sara began to rifle her purse. Almost absently, she added, "Or it could be someone you know."

The taste of carrot turned bitter in Lacey's mouth. "Someone I know? What are the odds of that?"

"Higher than you think. Here it is." She

produced a small, blue notebook and handed it to Lacey. "Don't get me wrong, I'm not saying it is an acquaintance of Celeste's, and therefore, by extension, you – it's just that statistically, most victims know their killers. I think that's why the police jumped on you so fast. But we can turn that to our advantage."

"How?"

"Well, for starters, Celeste wasn't exactly popular, right? You were practically her only friend. You knew her better than anyone. What I'd like you to do is to think of anybody and everybody who had contact with Celeste, and write their names in that little notebook. Any relationship at all. Barry's going to hire a detective to go over your list, and we'll see what turns up."

Shaking her head, Lacey said, "No one I could name would have wanted her dead."

"Don't worry about a motive. Just give me a list of people who were in her world. Can you do that for me?"

"I'll try." Lacey looked at the tablet. She flipped through the clean, white pages. "I don't know how many names I can come up with. Celeste didn't talk about people much."

"That just makes your job easier, doesn't it?" Snapping her purse shut, she said, "I feel terrible leaving you, but I really should run. Actually, if you'd rather I stay, I could make a few calls . . ."

"No, no. I'm okay. After Sean drove me here, I sent him home. I feel like being alone right now."

"All right then. By the way, Barry Cohen needs to set up a time to meet with you."

"I'll call him."

"Perfect. Okay, kiddo, I'll phone you the minute I'm finished. Mom's closing down the shop. I guess with the way things are right now, Kaleidoscope Jewels is history. Mrs Shephard won't even speak to Mom. She communicates only through her lawyer. Are you sure you're going to be okay?"

Lacey jumped from the couch and sprinted to the entryway. She opened the front door. "Go. *Go!*"

"You're sure?"

"Yes!"

"Don't let me forget my overnight bag. And, oh, there's a plate of food in the refrigerator. Mom'll be late. I'm locking this door so you'll be safe." Grabbing her bag, Sara leaned over and gave Lacey another squeeze. "Call if you need anything. Promise?"

"Promise."

From her living room window, Lacey watched as Sara hopped into her red Volkswagen. The car coughed and shuddered, almost as though it were indignant at the cold. Lacey didn't move until it disappeared around a bend in the road.

*   *   *

Steam filled the bathroom, condensing on the fixtures in tiny droplets. Her toe skimmed the top of the bathwater; it cut a path through the bubbles like a knife. Stepping in, Lacey let herself slide into the almost scalding water. The heat felt good. It purged the images of the casket, and the flowers, and Tamera from her mind.

The house was quiet, and for a moment, Lacey didn't move. She just drank in the stillness. In the jail, the noise never stopped. But the absence of sound was a sound in itself.

She eyed the notebook and pencil that lay on the edge of the tub. Okay, she told herself, I might as well get started. Who knew Celeste? Her teachers; that was obvious. Wiping her hands on a towel, she opened to the first page and wrote down the name of Celeste's teachers, beginning with first period. Morgan, Hernandez, Wykoff, she wrote. Giles, Steinman, Zowalski, Cameron. She set the pencil down and stared. A teacher? No way would any of them hurt Celeste. But I'm not supposed to worry about a motive, she reminded herself. Just make a list. Okay, who else?

Celeste's golden hair was always perfectly cut. Cathy McCune was her hairstylist. Cathy McCune, Lacey wrote down. Now who?

The first day they'd met, Celeste had mentioned her shrink. Had she ever said the name? Lacey concentrated, but came up blank. Beneath Cathy's name, Lacey drew a question mark. She bit her lip and let her mind wander through images of the kids at school. Tamera. Tamera knew Celeste. It gave her a small thrill of vengeance to scrawl Tamera Belmondi underneath the question mark. Lacey underlined it twice.

"Ever since you met Celeste, you've left me out of things," Tamera had complained. "It's like, she shows up and I'm out."

"That's not true," Lacey had countered. "We still do lots of stuff together. It's just, Celeste is new, and she's kind of shy."

"Shy, my butt! She's stuck-up. Whenever I try to talk to her, it's like," she'd made her voice high, "'I can't lower myself to talk to Tamera or any other children at Olympus High. My father is a diplomat. I'm far too mature.' Just watch her face the next time I talk to her. Yuck!"

"You're right, she needs a laxative, but you've got to remember that Celeste's hung around with adults a lot more than she has kids. Give her a chance."

Tamera had scowled. "I think it's rotten that you're responsible for her. Just because your mom and her mom are friends doesn't mean you and Celeste need to be joined at the hip. It's a stupid reason." She'd lifted her dark hair off her neck, then let it drop down her back. "Tell your mom she can be Celeste's friend, and then dump her. Dump Celeste, not your mom."

But Lacey hadn't dumped anyone. Instead, she'd tried to juggle everyone together. Occasionally, she'd managed to convince Celeste to share a cafeteria table with Tamera and Sean, and they'd made an uneasy bond that had lasted until the fight. After that, she and Tamera had just picked up where they left off, as if Celeste had never happened. It had become a threesome again, just Lacey, and Tamera, and Sean. Sean. She picked up the pencil, then set it down again. Sean had known Celeste. But not very well. He only knew her through their brief lunches. What was it Bernard Shephard had said about Sean at the church? Something about a mistake? She'd been so anxious to escape, his words had rolled off her.

She ran more hot water, swirled it through the tub and watched as the bubbles disappeared. Sean had never cared for Celeste, right? Then why did Bernard look at Sean and say – she tried to catch the words and string them together in her mind – "I realize you and Celeste were friendly, but you made a mistake in the end." The water felt suddenly cold. A mistake in the end? What could that mean?

"Get a grip, Lacey," she said out loud.

Sean, a killer. She ought to call him up and tell him. He'd probably be flattered. But doubts, unbidden, crept into her mind. Sean had broken into her house with his library card. That was strange. And that day, he'd told her he had dark thoughts. Could dark thoughts include murder?

No way! Lace, you're losing it. Sean won't even spray for spiders. Think of someone else.

Who did Celeste's nails? It was at the same salon . . .

But what could "a mistake in the end" mean? Had Sean seen Celeste without Lacey knowing? He wouldn't have. He, like Tamera, hadn't cared much for Celeste. Or had he?

Stop it. Stop thinking this way! Taking a deep breath, Lacey submerged herself completely. Hair floated around her like coils of seaweed. Opening her eyes, she saw the image of light play across the water, muted to a luminous glow. She gasped for air, then went under again. It was like being baptized, but instead of washing away her sins, she tried to wash away horrible thoughts. Suspended beneath the water, she could hear the rhythm of her heart, beating louder and faster. A little longer, a little longer . . . Finally bursting to the surface, Lacey took an enormous, gulping breath. Water ran from her hair and dripped into her bath like tears.

There was noise from downstairs. Rustling. Then silence.

Someone was in her house.

Grabbing a bath towel, she stepped from the tub and wrapped herself tightly. Maybe it was Sara, or her mother. Maybe she was hearing things. She slipped down the hall and stopped at the top of the stairs. A shadow passed through the entryway, and then she saw him.

Sean.

14

"Sean – what are you doing here?" Lacey shouted down the stairs.

"Hey, Lace, I thought you weren't here. I rang the bell and there was no answer. I brought you something."

"How did you get in?"

"Library card. I hope you don't mind—"

"Don't come any closer. I'm in a towel. Wait there until I get dressed."

She ran into her bedroom and slammed the door. Her bed was buried in stuffed animals; their glass eyes seemed to warn her. You're alone. He's in your house. He could be the killer. She yanked on her underwear. The quickest thing to put on was the black shirtdress she'd worn to the funeral.

She'd left it folded over the back of her chair. Her hands trembled as she fastened the six gold buttons. Did she hear something outside her door? Wrenching it open, she quickly looked out, but the hallway was empty.

"Do you mind if I get some milk?" Sean called up.

"Go ahead."

"Are you almost done up there?"

Instead of answering, Lacey appeared at the top of the stairs. She held on to the banister to keep her hand from shaking. Wet hair dampened her dress, deepening the color to coal.

"Come on down. I've got a surprise for you in the kitchen. What's wrong?" He stepped closer. Lacey tried to control an impulse to run. "You're still in black. That funeral really took something out of you, didn't it? Why are you stopping only halfway down the stairs? I'm not going to bite."

Sean had changed out of his suit. He wore only jeans and a gray T-shirt. His leather jacket hung on the doorknob behind him. He smiled at her; his teeth looked white.

"At the funeral, what did Bernard Shephard mean when he said you'd made a mistake in the end?" she asked.

"What?" The grin faded from his face.

"Bernard Shephard. Celeste's uncle." Lacey

gripped the banister. Her fingers felt wooden. "I've been thinking about what he said, and I can't figure it out. What did he mean?"

Shrugging, Sean said, "Nothing. I don't know. Come and see what I brought you."

Lacey didn't move. Glass brick bordered either side of the front door, and the western sunlight haloed him. But even though his features were shadowed, she could tell he had tensed.

"Did you ever see Celeste when I didn't know about it?"

His laughter was hollow. "What is this, the Inquisition? Why do you want to know?"

"It's a simple question. Did you ever see Celeste alone? What 'mistake' did you make? This isn't hard, Sean." Her voice came out louder than she intended. "Answer me!"

He narrowed his eyes, then dropped his gaze to the floor. Red flushed his cheeks and inched all the way down his neck. He studied the entryway tile intently, as if calculating a difficult equation. Finally, his eyes lifted.

"I saw Celeste the day she died. I went to her house to ask her a favor. She wouldn't do it. I left. She must have told her uncle I came by, but it was no big deal."

The blood stopped flowing to Lacey's legs. She sank to the step. "Did you hurt her?"

"*No!* How can you even ask me that?"

"Why didn't you tell me you were there? Why didn't you tell the police? How many secrets do you have?" Lacey's mind reeled. "My God, were you in love with her?"

"With Celeste? Are you crazy? I went to her house at five o'clock. I asked her if she'd step aside so you could keep your part in the dance recital. That's all. You were so freaked about losing that part. I wanted to help. I – I asked her if I could help her with all the classwork she'd missed. I told her I'd do it if she'd let you have that part. She said, 'No, I don't make deals anymore.' That was it. I went there for you. I did it for *you*!"

Her voice shook. In a half whisper, she asked, "What did you do for me?"

Sean stared at her, stunned. "You think I killed her?" A heartbeat later, he said flatly, "You think I killed her."

Lacey hesitated. How could she answer? It was as if her thoughts had become facets in a kaleidoscope. She couldn't sort them, make them focus in a pattern that made sense.

Grabbing his jacket from the door, Sean yanked it on. "I'm leaving now, Lacey. You stay up there, on the steps, where you can be safe from me. But I want you to think about something. When you were arrested, I never doubted you. I—" his voice cracked. He swallowed, then went on, "I didn't murder Celeste. If you don't believe me, ask my family. We went out to dinner and saw a play that night. I was out with my mother and father and brother until midnight."

"Sean—"

His hands shot up. "No! And I don't know what Bernard Shephard meant by that 'mistake in the end' crap. Maybe Celeste told him I tried to get her to drop out of the dance recital. Or maybe he just thought my big mistake was sitting in a church with *you*."

"Just wait, please—"

"Forget it, Lacey. You know what you need? You need to get some professional help. This thing is screwing up your mind. Until you get it together, don't call me, okay? I've believed in you. Maybe it's time you started believing in me."

The door banged shut behind him.

Almost as if she were in a dream, Lacey drifted down the stairs and into the kitchen. On the counter was a hastily scrawled note, and next to it were two Baskin-Robbins ice-cream cones, the kind with clown faces painted on. They were beginning to melt. The sugar cone hats had slipped to the side; the cherry noses pressed against their frosting smiles, causing them to droop off-center. Lacey picked up the note. It read,

> *Dear Lacey,*
> *Sorry I missed you – but I wanted to bring*

you a treat. Check the refrigerator for Bozo and friend, and while you eat, smile! *Seriously, though, I want you to know that I'll always be here for you, no matter—*

The note stopped there.

She let the paper slip through her fingers. It spun to the floor like an autumn leaf dropping from a branch. Heaving sobs raked through her. How could she have accused Sean? What was wrong with her? Now he was hurt and angry, and might never forgive her. And whose fault would that be? Would she be looking at everyone from now on as if they could be killers? She began to shiver; her breath became shallow; the room seemed to tilt. Sean was right, she needed help. Her mother? No, her mother was in the middle of dismembering her business, and she was already on edge. Sara was gone. She stared at the phone. All of her friends at school, and yet, who could she call? If Tamera had rejected her, they all would.

Hands trembling, she found Otkin's number in the Rolodex and pushed the buttons for his office.

"I – I need to see Mr Otkin. It's, I'm Lacey Brighton."

"This is his answering service. The office is closed. Do you have an appointment?" a sterile voice asked.

"No." It was hard to speak; her throat felt as if

it had been caught in a vise. "No," she repeated. "But would you please tell him Lacey Brighton needs to talk to him today. Can you call him? *Please!*"

"One moment."

Muzak floated around her, like a syrupy cloud. The voice clicked back on. "Miss Brighton, Mr Otkin said to tell you to come right in. He's at his office now, but was about to leave. Can you come right away?"

"Yes."

"Do you have a way to get there?"

"I've got my car."

"Good. There's an entrance on the north side. He said to use that door, which will take you up some stairs and into a small reception room in the back. He'll take you to his office from there. All right?"

"Thank you. Tell him . . . thanks."

She hung up the phone, then grabbed her purse and her coat. Her shoes had been left by the front door; even though she had no panty hose, she slipped on the shoes. She had to hurry! Her eyes rested on the ice-cream clowns. Carefully, she put them into the freezer and gently shut the door. She'd wait to eat hers until she and Sean could do it together.

"Lacey, it's so good to see you. I've heard about

your hard times since we did the hypnosis. My office is right this way. You've never been through the back, have you?"

"No. Thank you for seeing me on a Saturday, Mr Otkin. I know it's your day off. It's just, I really needed to talk to you."

"Relax. I was here doing paperwork. Believe me, there's no problem at all." He fumbled with some keys and said, "Let me just unlock this door. I've been in my office already, but I needed to do some copying down the hall and I locked it from habit. Here we go." He dropped the key into his pocket and flipped on the lights. "Why don't you have a seat? I'll pull my chair around."

The blinds were shut, and the office was dim. The whole building was closed down for the weekend, as if problems had no business appearing on a Saturday. It seemed a lifetime since Lacey had told Otkin about her nightmares, and about Sara, and all of her fears. If only her life were that simple again. If only her problems were small, instead of the crushing ones that seemed as though they'd kill her.

"Let me take your coat. You just sit." He took her navy-blue parka, hung it on a hook behind the door. "I heard about the police twisting your dream into a confession. Terrible," he clucked. "Just terrible. I'm sure justice will prevail, and you'll be found innocent. You're tensing, Lacey. Take a cleansing breath. That's the way. What can I help you with today?"

Her chest tightened. "A little while ago, I accused someone I really care about of murder."

"Oh?" Otkin looked nonplussed. "Who?"

"My boyfriend, Sean. Sean says I need help, and he's right. I think I'm losing it. He's been really good to me, and for a while I thought he might have done it. What am I going to think next? My mom's a killer? My sister? I've got this – this desperation to find out who killed Celeste, but," she choked with emotion, "I can't start accusing people I love. What's wrong with me?"

"Nothing's wrong with you. As usual, you're far too hard on yourself." Soothingly, Otkin said, "What made you suspect Sean?"

"Sara said to make a list of everyone who knew Celeste, and give it to her so a detective could investigate. While I was writing the names down, I thought of Sean, and just for a second I said, 'Wait a minute, maybe it's him.' I asked Sean if he killed Celeste." She started to cry. "And now he hates me. I don't blame him."

Instead of his usual slacks and sweater, Otkin wore a velour, chocolate-colored jogging suit. He looked rounder and softer than Lacey remembered, almost like a teddy bear. Rolling his chair to his desk, he plucked a small box of tissues off the edge of his desk and handed it to her. "Lacey, what you're doing is completely normal. You've been through an incredible trauma. You've experienced things that would destroy most adults. Give yourself some room. You know, you are your own worst enemy."

Pulling a tissue, she rubbed under her eyes, then blew her nose. "I feel so messed up inside. We, Sean and I, went to Celeste's funeral today. Celeste's uncle came up and made me leave. I thought I was going to die. Then Sara said, 'There's an easy way out of this, Lacey, if we find the real killer.' Then I was by myself and Sean came in—"

"Whoa, back up. Where was Sara?"

"She'd already left."

"Your mother wasn't there?"

"No, she's packing up Kaleidoscope Jewels – she's lost her business because of me! Everything is such a mess. So I was taking a bath, and Sean let himself into my house with his library card and—"

"Slow down, Lacey. I can't follow what you're saying. Remember to breathe. That's the way. First of all, does your mother know you're in my office?"

"No. I called and your answering service told me to come right in, so I just got my stuff and left as fast as I could."

He rested his hands on his knees. "All right. Now let's think of the steam and the hot soup.

Inhale, exhale. Blow away that steam." His voice was serene, calm. "Try to close your eyes. If you don't want to do that, focus on the flowers."

The melon blossoms must have died. They had been replaced with a spray of silk violets. Lacey concentrated on the tiny purple bouquet. Other than the flowers, his office was exactly as it had always been. The familiar books, the sand-colored carpet, the softened light. This is what she needed. A place where feelings could mute into ivory walls.

"Tell me about the list your sister wants you to write."

"It's just names of everyone who knew Celeste. Some detective is going to go over it."

"You wrote down Sean's name?"

She nodded.

"You thought Sean was capable of murder?"

"No – yes. Maybe. That's why I'm here. I'm so mixed up! I can't go around thinking everyone could murder. I can't live that way! I feel like I'm watching someone else in my body, you know? It's like it's not me anymore." She twisted the Kleenex into a rope.

"Take me back to the beginning. Try to let the anxiety flow from you as you speak. What happened after the funeral?"

"Okay, I was in the bathtub, and Sean rang the bell. I didn't hear it, though. I guess it was because I was underwater."

Lacey flashed on an image of Celeste. The day she'd gone to tell her about the dance recital.

"What is it, Lacey? What are you thinking?"

"You know what's a strange coincidence?" Her words came more slowly, deliberately. "The day I had the fight with Celeste, she was in the bathtub, too. Only I kept ringing the bell, and then, when she didn't answer, I threw snowballs at her window until she came down." She paused, and frowned. "Don't you think that's kind of strange? I mean Celeste was in the tub, and she didn't hear her doorbell, and then I was in the tub, and I didn't hear mine?"

"I don't see a connection . . ."

"I just thought of something else that's kind of odd."

"Can you tell me?"

"Well, when Celeste came to the door, she said she'd just gotten out of the tub. But she couldn't have. Now that I think about it, her hair was completely dry."

"Was it pulled up? In a barrette, perhaps?"

"No, it was down. Her hair was long. At least the ends should have been wet. I've got to think. Something about that day doesn't make sense."

"You're tensing. Try to concentrate, Lacey."

"It's like it's there, but I can't catch it. I don't know."

"Visualize. Visualize that time with Celeste.

Detach yourself. Look at the surroundings as though your eye is a camera. What do you see?"

Lacey hesitated. "Gold – there was gold around her neck, and she had on a watch. I can almost see it. It had a tiny chain that hung beside the clasp." She squeezed her eyes shut. "If she were taking a bath, she wouldn't have had that watch on. Or her necklace."

"Go on."

"There was something at the bottom of the banister. I remember brushing against it when I was leaving."

"Did you hear anything? A voice, perhaps? Sean's voice?"

"No. Wait. It was a coat, sort of hanging over the banister at the bottom of their stairs. A man's coat. I can't believe I didn't think of this before."

His voice softened. "Sean? It was Sean's coat?"

"No. His is a brown leather bomber jacket. This one was long, like an overcoat."

Otkin rolled his chair closer. "Could it have been her father's? A brother's, perhaps?"

Pressing her fingers into her forehead, Lacey said, "No. Her parents were gone, and she doesn't have a brother. This was camel-colored, maybe cashmere. It had a scarf, with a strange plaid, kind of gray and green. I can see it!"

The kaleidoscope turned; she could see the picture.

"Someone was there that day, with her, at the house! A man. I've got to tell Sara – this could be important!"

"Your breathing is shallow, Lacey. I don't think this is as significant as you believe it to be. You're looking for another easy escape. We should stay and deal with your feelings—"

"You don't understand!" Lacey's eyes snapped open. Leaping to her feet, she cried, "I missed what was going on there. That's why Celeste was so bizarre – someone was with her, and she didn't want me to know! She wasn't dressed – all she had on was a robe, so if there was a man there . . ."

"It could have been another teenager."

"No way. That was no kid's coat. I've got to go. I've got to tell Sara!"

Otkin stood. "Be calm. Put your shoes on. Let me get your parka for you—"

"I'll grab it—"

She turned and yanked her parka off the hook on the back of Otkin's door. Beneath it was a coat. A man's camel-colored coat, with a gray-and-green plaid scarf.

15

Before she could move, Otkin was there. He placed one hand against the door, then pulled his keys from his pocket and quickly locked it. The overcoat swayed slightly against the back of the door.

"I'm so sorry you had to see my coat. It's very unfortunate."

The coat. It was the same coat that had been at Celeste's home. Otkin had been with Celeste that day. Lacey had to pretend she didn't know – try to act as if she hadn't seen. She took a deep breath. Behave like it never happened, she told herself. Pretend what you see isn't real.

"So – I'd better fly." Her voice sounded strange in her ears. "Sara's waiting for me. I told Sara I was here, and she said to come over the minute I was done talking to you. Thank you so much for everything. You've been wonderful."

"Sara doesn't know you're here. No one does. Lacey, come and sit down. We aren't done yet."

Even though he was only inches away, Lacey couldn't look into his eyes. The eyes of a killer.

His hand landed firmly on her shoulder to push her toward her chair. She could feel his fingers bore into her back, but his voice had the same, even tone as always. "Please. Sit."

"I need to leave—"

"Sit." This time it was a command.

The door is locked. The building is empty. Oh, God! Lacey thought.

"You should have let me get your coat. I offered, but you are so impulsive. I can't tell you how this distresses me. Stay in your chair." He walked to his desk and opened the center drawer. He pulled out a polished letter opener and held it to his eyes, flashing its eight-inch blade in the light. "I don't know if this is sharp enough. What do you think?"

She stared, her mind refusing to sort out the information that was there. Otkin held a blade in his hand. The coat was his. She was alone. She was going to die.

"Remember your breathing, Lacey. You look as if you're leaving me. Just listen to how shallow your breath is."

"I – I don't understand."

Otkin shook his head. "No, I don't suppose you do. Celeste never told you, did she?" Reaching into the drawer, he pulled out a stack of letters.

"Told me what?"

"About us. She swore she spoke to no one, but I was never completely sure. You were right, Lacey. Someone was in her house that day. I was there. I saw you, and I watched you throw those ridiculous snowballs."

Lacey's mind reeled.

"Celeste was very special to me. We were in love. From the moment she became my patient, I knew she was something extraordinary. She was a gamine, half woman, half child. But then, that day you came to her home and told her about that inane recital, Celeste told me she couldn't live a double life anymore. She said she had to leave, and be by herself and think. That night, she packed her bags and left."

His face darkened. Returning to his chair, he sat facing Lacey. He picked up an envelope, and withdrew a piece of lavender paper. Lacey was close enough to smell the lilac scent of Celeste's stationery.

"She wrote me this while she was away." His tortoiseshell glasses hung from his neck. Slipping them on, he held the page in front of him, as if he were about to present an essay from a student.

"'Glade,

Now that I am away from you, I see things for what they are. You have abused me, mentally and physically.'"

The door, Lacey thought. If I can just reach the door . . .

He peered over the page, and looked at her sternly. "I would appreciate it if you would not move, even a muscle," he told her. "There is nothing you can do. The door is locked from the inside, and the windows are sealed. Please, concentrate on what I'm saying. I want you to listen to what Celeste says about me." He cleared his throat.

"'Glade, it's obvious that you don't love me. You have only used me, and I can never let that happen again.'"

He looked at Lacey almost as if he were pleading. "I could understand that she wanted to break away from me. I knew it couldn't last. But she took our relationship and cheapened it. And *here*" – he smacked the page – "here is where she goes too far. Listen to this.

'You might think I will just fade from your life but I cannot do that. I won't. Because if I don't bring what you did to me into the light, you will do it again to someone else in the dark. And I

believe I owe something to the next young victim. I will not let another girl's youth be stolen from her, the way you savaged mine from me.'

"Savaged?" His voice was incredulous. "I helped her. I gave her maturity, and this is how I was repaid." He ran his finger down the page, muttering, until he cried, "Ah, here it is. Consider how she closes her letter.

'When my parents get back from Hong Kong, I will tell them everything. You will never steal another soul again.'"

He took off his glasses and let them hang from his neck. His hand rested on the letter opener, fingering its edge.

"She mentioned you a lot, you know. She said you were her only real friend. She liked the way you made her laugh."

Lacey's mouth was so dry she could hardly get the words out. "Why? Why did you kill her?"

"I just told you. She was going to go public with our affair. It would have meant humiliation, the end of my practice – jail! You, of all people, should realize what a horrifying thought jail is! I went to her house that night, to plead with her to reconsider. She was alone. I knew her parents would arrive the next day." He turned the opener in his hand, like a worry stone. "She was cutting material for a costume. I said, 'Celeste, you can't do this.' She looked at me, but her eyes had changed. Those beautiful, beautiful eyes. It was as if I had become the enemy. 'I'll do what I have to,' she told me. And then I said, 'So will I.'"

He shook his head, as if to clear his thoughts. "I must say, your nightmare became a very unnerving twist for me. What you saw in your dream was a mirror of what happened to Celeste that night."

Wagging his finger at her, he said, "When I had you under hypnosis, I thought any second you would say, 'I see the face of the killer! It's Glade Otkin!' But you never quite focused on the face." He looked at her, and grinned. "You can see it now, can't you?"

"Yes."

"You're not breathing, Lacey. Try to relax."

"I can't – I – what happens now?"

"That is an interesting question. I wasn't prepared for such a turn of events. Ah, well, I can improvise." He looked off into the distance. "Twelve years ago, one of my patients, another teenager like you, disappeared. They found his car at the bus depot, but Jerod never turned up. That always intrigued me, the way the police and family assumed he ran away."

He tapped the letter opener against his knee. "He was never heard from again, but to this very day, his parents believe he'll come back. Pathetic, really."

Lacey's eyes were riveted to his face. He looked so different, so cold, unfeeling.

"I'll drive your car to the depot and leave it there. I'm confident they'll come to the same conclusion about you."

"On a bus? Where would I go?"

Suddenly, he focused on her. "You misunderstand." His voice became deep. "You're not going anywhere."

Lacey's insides turned to water. She had to play chess with this man, and maneuver for time. For her life. "The woman from the answering service knows I'm here."

"I doubt she'd say anything about our appointment. If she does, I can simply say you never showed up. She won't present a problem."

"If I die, my family will never stop looking for my killer. They'll hire an investigator. They'll never let it go!"

"I agree. Absolutely. If you turned up dead, there'd be questions. The police might even reopen Celeste's case, and that would be risky. No, it would be ideal if you simply vanished. You see, it's entirely logical that faced with a murder charge, you'd bolt. I already told the police you were unstable. Privately, I said you were violent, capable of murder. They'll have no trouble believing you'd run. Trust me."

He stood. Methodically, he walked to the door and removed his coat from the hook. "We'll do this at the bottom of the stairwell. Blood on my carpet could prove difficult to explain." He draped his coat over his left arm. "Celeste struggled, and believe me, Lacey, that made it so much harder. Remember to use your relaxing techniques. They will help you in the moments to come. Put on your shoes."

"God! You can't just kill me! Please!" She was gasping, choking on her own pleas for mercy. "Please, don't do this!"

"I'm sorry, Lacey. There is a single course left to me. As with the laws of physics, there can only be one outcome."

The laws of physics, the laws of physics. The phrase raced through her mind. Something was there, a way out. She looked at the floor where her shoes stood side by side. What was it? Pressure equals force. Sean had told her. Pressure equals force divided by area. A law of physics. Her shoes lay at her feet. Terror made her mind work with uncommon clarity.

Otkin shifted the blade from his right hand to his left. He dug through his pocket for his keys.

"Your shoes," he told her. "Hurry."

Her fingers gripped the body of one shoe. For an instant, Otkin took his eyes off her as he fumbled in his pocket.

Clutching her high-heeled pump, she stood. Arm down her back, as though holding a tennis racket poised for a serve, she charged him. She had only one shot. One way out.

She swung the shoe – rage gave her strength. The narrow point of the heel smashed against his temple; the side of Otkin's head seemed to explode. Blood sprayed her in tiny droplets.

Again. Over her head, then down. He dropped to his knees. She clubbed him again. With each smash, she gave a cry. The impact shook her arm, wrenching her shoulder. Again. Not counting the blows, Lacey struck him. His eyes widened with shock.

Clawing the air, he lunged for her. His hands gripped her dress and he sank onto the floor. Blood seeped from his head as he toppled over.

The door was locked.

"Please!" she screamed. Pounding against it, she shrieked *"Somebody help me!"*

It was quiet. Empty. Her heart banged wildly in her chest. Otkin lay stomach-down. His hair, usually so meticulously combed, flared onto the floor in a mat of blood. The keys were still in his hand. The keys. She had to have the keys.

"Oh, God, oh, God, oh, God," Lacey cried, moving closer to where Otkin lay. Trembling furiously, she plucked the keys from his palm, then returned to the door. Ten keys. Her hands shook so violently she could barely get the tip of the first key into the lock.

Otkin groaned.

Lacey, eyes wide with horror, glanced from the door to Otkin. "Don't move. I'll hurt you!" Her voice was shrill. "Don't make me hit you again!"

The second key was wrong. The chain dropped between her fingers and onto the floor, just feet away from him. When she squatted to grab them, Otkin flinched. Slowly, he began to pull himself up. He stared at her. Blood poured from a gash into his mouth.

Shallow, ragged breathing, so loud it filled the room. It came from Lacey. Don't panic, she commanded herself. Breathe. Take the key. Concentrate. Put it in the lock. Turn. Breathe.

The lock clicked. Flinging open the door, she grabbed her purse and raced barefoot through the hallway, down the stairs and out into the snow-packed parking lot. The cold air knifed her lungs. It hurt to breathe. The pain never left until her car had backed onto the street.

16

Lacey sat curled on the couch and stared out of their living room window. Her arm rested along the couch's back, and her chin dug into the rise of her shoulder.

It was the fifth of March, and it looked as if spring was about to break. Green-fringed branches pressed against the window, etching an ornamental pattern against the sky. A dog barked in the distance. On the sidewalk, a boy approached on his bike. The rhythmic clicking of a card in his spokes swelled, then faded as he disappeared down the street.

Lacey felt hollow inside. It was as if her body ate, and moved, and did all the right things, but her soul had left it. The old Lacey Brighton was as cold and dead as Celeste.

A red Volkswagen puttered up the street and swung into their driveway. Sara hopped out with her briefcase; her purse bounced against her hip as she made her way up the front walk. Lacey heard the sound of a key in the front door.

"I'm here," Sara called brightly. "How are you doing?"

"Okay."

"I've only got a minute – I'm due back in court. Mom said to give you a squeeze. She'll be home by six."

A cloud of cool air followed Sara inside. She was back in her law uniform; gray crepe suit, silk blouse, pearls. Dropping her briefcase onto the floor, she sat beside Lacey on the couch.

"On my way here, I stopped in at Kaleidoscope Jewels. Elaine Shephard talked to Mom today. She's selling her share of the business."

"What does Mom think?"

"I don't know. It's going to be hard, but I guess it will work out. Do you realize Elaine is the one who told Mom that Otkin would be a great therapist for you?"

A shudder passed through Lacey. "Really?"

"Yes. When Mom mentioned how stressed you were, Elaine told her that she should take you to Otkin. She said he was wonderful, the absolute best. But Elaine never once said that Celeste was in therapy. I guess even though she and Mom shared a business, Elaine couldn't admit that her daughter wasn't perfect. Unbelievable."

"Celeste never said a word about him. I guess the Shephards really know how to keep secrets." Lacey began to twist her hair into a rope.

"How are your nightmares?"

"Better. Last night, I dreamed I hit the man in the ski mask back. I guess I'm making progress."

"That's good. Has Sean been by today?"

Sean. Lacey managed a tiny smile.

"I'll take that as a yes," Sara said.

After Otkin had been taken away in an ambulance, after Lacey had been interviewed and re-interviewed, after the charges against her had been dropped, her mother had driven her home. Sean had been at the edge of their driveway, sitting in his car, waiting. He'd not said a word, just walked to her and hugged her as hard as he could. Her mother had started to cry, but Lacey hadn't. She just clung to Sean, and smelled him, and knew that everything between them was all right.

"Sean had to leave for band practice," she told Sara now, "but he'll be back this evening. He's tutoring me."

"In what?" Sara touched Lacey's arm lightly. "Love?"

"No, schoolwork. I've got a lot of studying ahead of me. I need to catch up."

"Wonderful." Taking her hand, Sara said, "Really,

that's great. I'll help you in any way I can."

Shaking her head softly, Lacey looked through the window into the sky.

"What? What is it?"

"I've been sitting here thinking. Everyone out there just comes and goes. I was watching the Gilmours unload their groceries, and I thought, They think their lives are all ordered, like the next day is for sure going to be the same as the last. But – I . . ." She stared at Sara. "No one knows how much time they've got. I mean, for me, I realize that I can't waste my life screwing around, because tomorrow might never come."

Sara shrugged. "You can't obsess about it. It's the same for everybody. You do your best, and go on."

"But before I die, I want to do something. To *be* something."

"You already are, Lacey."

"No. I'm not! Celeste didn't get the chance to live her life. I almost didn't get the chance. And if I *had* died, you know how I would have been remembered?" She punched the air with her finger, "Here lies Lacey Brighton; she told a great joke."

"That's not true. And even if it were, I can think of worse things."

"It's not enough!" Lacey insisted. "I've still got time to get serious. Otkin almost killed me. But he didn't. Now I just want to fix everything I did wrong. I want to do it over. Better." She looked at the floor. The bottom of Sara's briefcase was scuffed.

"I want you to listen to me, Lacey. I've got some news for you, good news. Otkin's pleaded guilty. With Celeste's murder and an additional charge of attempted murder against him, he's looking at hard time. Twenty-five years to life."

Without making a sound, Lacey mouthed, "Thank God."

"You're safe now. Otkin's confessed, spring is coming, life is good. Don't let him take your sparkle away."

Sara hesitated. Her eyes went from Lacey to her briefcase. "I think I want to show you something." From the bottom of her briefcase she produced a manila folder. She drew out some xeroxed sheets and set them on the coffee table in front of her.

"What are they?" Lacey asked. "Court papers?"

"No. They're letters, copies of the letters Celeste wrote to Otkin. I only have the pages that mention you."

Pressing her lips together, Lacey shut her eyes, then opened them. "Put them back."

"My friend is prosecuting Otkin, and she let me see them. I really believe you need to read what Celeste wrote about you."

"No." Lacey shook her head harder.

Sara sighed a long sigh and stood. "I understand how you feel. It's only been a week, and the wounds are still fresh. But there are some things Celeste said that might make you heal faster."

Snapping her briefcase shut, she declared, "This may be a mistake, but I'm going to leave the copies here. If you toss them in the garbage, fine. It's your decision. You choose."

She leaned over and kissed the top of Lacey's head. "I love you, kiddo. Take care, now."

It was nearing dusk before Lacey picked up the first page from the coffee table. Celeste's beautiful scrolled writing looped across the page. The xerox made her writing bolder, but it was Celeste's. Lacey ran her finger along the lines. It only took her an instant to find her name.

You have taught me a lot, Glade, and you are my best friend, besides Lacey. Sometimes, I really wish I could tell her. Of course, I never will. I'll honor our vow until the day I die. But there are times when I can tell she wonders about me, and I feel so cut off from her. I can never explain to her why I act the way I do. And you are wrong about her sense of humor. Of course it's silly, but she and I are only seventeen. When else can we laugh? You never seem to. I only feel young when I'm with her.

Lacey's hand shook as she turned to the next page.

Do you know what Lacey asked today? "What's brown and black and looks good on a lawyer? A Doberman!" I was sitting next to her in the school cafeteria, and everyone at our table started to laugh. I thought, I wished, I could be like she is. It's as if she eats up life. She tastes it, and loves it, and enjoys it. I just watch. I wonder if I can learn.

Another page.

Lacey and I went to the mall, and she tried on this outrageous outfit, and the saleswoman started to joke with her. I hate it when that happens, Glade. I become invisible. I no longer exist. I stand to the side, and watch, and curse that I'm not more like she is. How can some people make friends wherever they go, and I can't even be friends with the one I have?

Lacey let the letters fall into her lap. Tears rose to her eyes, then stopped.

Celeste's legacy lay in her hands.

About the Author

Alane Ferguson says, "The real world of crime and law both frightens and fascinates me. My research has convinced me that I never want to be on the wrong side of a cell door."

The author lives in Sandy, Utah.

POINT HORROR
Read if you dare. . . .

Are you hooked on horror? Are you thrilled by fear? Then these are the books for you. A powerful series of horror fiction designed to keep you quaking in your shoes.

Also in the Point Horror series:

The Waitress
by Sinclair Smith

Look out for:

The Window
by Carol Ellis

The Fever
by Diane Hoh

Hit and Run
by R.L. Stine

The Train
by Diane Hoh

Beach House
by R.L. Stine

The Perfume
by Caroline B. Cooney

P●INT CRiME

If you like Point Horror, you'll love Point Crime!

A murder has been committed . . . Whodunnit?
Was it the teacher, the schoolgirl, or the best friend? An
exciting new series of crime novels, with tortuous plots and
lots of suspects, designed to keep the reader guessing till
the very last page.

School for Death
Peter Beere
When the French teacher is found, drowned in the pond,
Ali and her friends are plunged into a frightening night-
mare. Murder has come to Summervale School, and
anyone could be the next victim . . .

Shoot the Teacher
David Belbin
Adam Lane, new to Beechwood Grange, finds himself
thrust into the middle of a murder investigation, when the
headteacher is found shot dead. And the shootings have
only just begun . . .

The Smoking Gun
Malcolm Rose
When David Rabin is found dead, in the school playing-
field, his sister Ros is determined to find the murderer. But
who would have killed him? And why?

Look out for:

Baa Baa Dead Sheep
Jill Bennett
Mr Lamb, resident caretaker of the *Tree Theatre*, has been
murdered, and more than one person at the theatre had
cause to hate him . . .

Avenging Angel
David Belbin
When Angelo Coppola is killed in a hit-and-run accident,
his sister, Clare, sets out to find his killer . . .

Point Romance

Anyone can hear the language of love.

Are you burning with passion, and aching with desire? Then these are the books for you! Point Romance brings you passion, romance, heartache, and most of all, *love* . . .

Saturday Night
Caroline B. Cooney

Summer Dreams, Winter Love
Mary Francis Shura

The Last Great Summer
Carol Stanley

Last Dance
Caroline B. Cooney

Cradle Snatcher
Alison Creaghan

Look out for:

New Year's Eve
Caroline B. Cooney

French Kiss
Robyn Turner

Kiss Me, Stupid
Alison Creaghan

Summer Nights
Caroline B. Cooney